NEARLY A MURDER

A VIOLET CARLYLE HISTORICAL MYSTERY NOVEL

BETH BYERS

SUMMARY

July 1926

Violet and Jack have determined upon an adventure. In a moment of sheer madness, they and their friends find room on a steamship leaving the country and board without even being certain of where they're going.

One would think that would be the oddest thing about their trip. Only soon into the trip, two women are discovered unconscious. It seems that they've both been poisoned. But whoever has poisoned them chose a different poison for each. Who is this mad poisoner and when will they strike again?

CHAPTER 1

"Where do you want to go?" Rita asked, her sapphire blue eyes wide with a joy that reflected her love of traveling.

One might not imagine that the golden-haired, elegant, high-fashioned Rita was such an adventuress, but it was easy for her to set aside her pearls and her high-heeled shoes for something meant for a safari or a jungle.

Until Vi met Rita, Vi had considered herself something of a world traveler. She'd learned better since those early days. Even still, Vi felt the same flash of excitement. It wasn't so much the taking of a trip that was unusual for them, but the suddenness of it. They'd considered going back to London when Jack's casual aside opened up the idea of anywhere in the world.

"Morocco?" Rita tried to ask casually. "Oh! America?"

Vi hid a snort when she saw Rita's heel bouncing despite her attempt at a casual tone. Of them all, Rita had a passion for seeing and experiencing the world that left the rest as permanent dilettantes.

"Cuba," Victor suggested immediately. "I could use more rum."

"We can buy rum here," Kate told him, with the casual cruelty of a wife who knew exactly how much rum he had in their stuffed cellars.

"I like to buy it myself." Victor's unoffended ease with Kate's aside showed when he lifted her hand and kissed the back of it. "Are you up to traveling, love?"

"I think so," Kate replied, letting her hand drop onto where their next baby was growing. "I shouldn't like to be left behind."

Vi had to agree. The first time Kate had been expecting, she'd been so ill that Violet still shuddered at the memory. And to be honest with herself, Kate's illness was one of the major reasons why Vi was so careful about avoiding pregnancy herself. This last pregnancy, however, Kate had an experienced nanny who knew exactly what to do to keep Kate from constantly sicking up. She was still ill, just not to a debilitating extent.

"The Amalfi coast?" Jack asked.

They were known to slip down to the Italian coast, enjoy the villa that Aunt Agatha had left to Vi, and then slip home. Rita and Vi shook their heads in unison. The villa was a home away from home. It was their version of a hunting or fishing cabin.

"That's not adventurous enough," Vi said as she leaned back. "Not now. Dreaming has taken over, and we're going exotic, I think, darling."

They were in Rita and Ham's home in the country and had ended up moving into the same house even though Victor and Kate, as well as Vi and Jack, had their own country homes. Lila and Denny only had a London home, but they almost always stayed with Jack and Vi when they were in the country. "What about a train ride to somewhere exciting? The kind with those sleeping cabins and little sitting rooms? We haven't done that yet."

Ham lifted a brow and glanced at his wife. She was excited, but she was also the person who had the most experience. As a near-professional traveler, she was the hardest to satisfy. Violet watched Ham weigh the wants of his wife, and she was curious how he would vote.

He rubbed the back of his neck and then smoothed his beard before he said, "Or—"

With a long pause, Lila finally stepped in and asked, "Or?"

"Or, we could just pack our trunks flexibly, go to a port, and buy tickets on the first steamship that has room for us."

Rita blinked rapidly, but Vi could see the excitement growing in her friend's sapphire eyes.

"Just anywhere?" Rita asked. "We wouldn't be prepared. We wouldn't have a guide book or even a hotel when we get there."

"Rita, darling," Ham told her easily. "You've taught me that ready money provides a bit of power to get the things you desire."

She paused, flushing slightly at his sardonic tone, but her eyes were wide as she imagined something lovely. Ham wasn't wrong, Vi thought. Since she and her twin, Victor, had transformed from the working nobility into fortunate heirs, they'd experienced both ends of the financial spectrum. They had moved from oddly smelling little rooms to mansions, and she rather thought she had a unique perspective because of it. The truth was, with their allowance, she and Victor had never had to work that hard. They'd written their books to supplement their income and lived on more omelets and cans of sardines than one would otherwise desire, but they'd been happy.

If anything, Vi thought, glancing at her twin, she struggled harder with more money than less. They'd come in contact with so many people who were willing to do *anything* for a fortune that they felt as though they'd been cursed with their lives being infected by murderers. Those murderers had left Vi struggling with grey days that she battled the best as she could.

"He's not wrong," Denny added, rubbing his hands together. "Lila and I aren't drowning in the bullion like you fortunate few, but even we could probably arrange a hotel room wherever we go."

"So," Rita said, "we'd need party dresses but also sturdy trousers and comfortable boots." Her eyes lit up. "Should we bring a fishing pole or furs, it's almost impossible to know. I've never been to so many places. What if there's somewhere that is just…life changing?"

"I understand that Rio de Janeiro is exciting. It's near a beach with beautiful oceans, casinos, probably endless parties," Ham suggested easily. It was clear he didn't really care where they went. "I believe there are rather frequent ships there."

"What about that pirate island? We've almost gone there a few times. Tortuga?" This was from Denny, who looked as though he were nine years old again and having pirate adventures of his own.

"What about the surprise?" Rita begged. "Oh, please. That does sound rather more exciting than anything else."

"Let's do that then," Vi agreed when no one objected. "We won't be able to build up our hopes and then be disappointed. It'll be like…like…sleuthing out the best places to see, eat, dance, play."

"Yes!" Rita cheered. "I need a drink." Her gaze turned to Victor and she begged, "Please? One of those blackberry ones?"

"As long as we don't rule out Cuba if that's the first option, I'm happy enough with that plan," Victor agreed, rising to cross to their little bar and pour drinks for the lot of them.

Kate shrugged when Rita's gaze turned to her. She was the easiest of their group, save Lila who was too lazy to care about much more than being with her family. With Denny and their daughter Lily, she'd be happy in London, Tortuga, or Rio. Especially if there was dancing, excellent food, and a comfortable place for a good nap.

"Bloody hell," Denny muttered, "how will I pack enough chocolate if we don't end up in Europe?"

"I'm sure almost anywhere in the world has chocolate," Lila teased. "It doesn't even come from here, darling."

"Lila, you don't understand my need for chocolate. Good chocolate."

"The only thing I know about your desperation for chocolate is that it turns your mid-section soft and equals Vi's need for Turkish coffee. You're a bit beastly without your chocolate, my lad."

Ham laughed and said, "That's a need I have as well, now. Shall we pack carefully to bring that along?"

"I say we start right now," Rita said. "Let's roll the dice on train versus steamships and start from there."

Vi examined her trunk and then glanced at her husband. He'd packed already, and she scowled at him. His broad grin was even more irritating. She turned and jumped onto his smirking self and then grabbed his cheeks like he was a baby. She smooshed them together pulling another laugh from him and then pouted, "It's harder for me to pack. Remember when I had Beatrice, and she took good care of me?"

"I do. It is terribly harder for you to pack," he agreed easily and then laughed when she pinched him for teasing her. He laughed again and then tried, "You have all those underthings and jewels and your collection of kimonos. However will you be as spoiled as you are if you have to limit yourself to a mere multitude of trunks?"

Vi gasped and then smacked his cheek lightly. "Not nice."

He laughed again and settled his hands on her hips. "What if you just packed one kimono?"

"But what will I wear while the first is being cleaned?"

"Nothing?" he suggested lightly, and she smacked him again. When that didn't work, she tried for a tickle, but she was the one who ended up gasping and twisting while he won the tickle war.

"Mercy!" she begged.

"Where do you want to go?"

Jack considered and Vi took the moment to examine his face. It was roughly hewn and the epitome of handsome, though she knew that many women preferred the smooth features of her twin or the affable cheeriness of Denny. But for Vi, it was Jack. He was one of the largest men Vi knew, with broad shoulders and a wide chest. She examined it and then decided to lean on him. She pressed her ear next to his heart and listened to her favorite lullaby.

Jack trailed his hand up and down her spine until they heard the dinner gong, and they both laughed. Jack was ready, of course, but Vi needed to drop her evening gown over her slip and add her favorite red lipstick. She scurried through finishing dressing, but they were still too late for the early cocktails.

Somehow, however, when dinner was finished, she was slightly zozzled. A part of her wondered if she should wait for the morning to pack, but she guessed Rita would be ready to go at the crack of dawn. Vi made her selections, with Jack saving her from forgetting stockings and shoes, and then helping her choose evening gowns by randomly pulling some out and telling her he'd loved her in those dresses in particular.

Vi gasped, "I haven't worn two of those!"

"I'm just remembering some future evening," he said with a flicker of a lash or an adjustment of his expression. "It's a bit difficult to differentiate between forecasted memories and experienced memories."

Vi leaned back, stumbled a little and put her hands on her hips, and then couldn't help but laugh. "So what you're saying is that you don't care what dresses I wear?"

"Not at all, darling," Jack told her easily and this time his gaze roved over her as he smiled slightly. "Though I do have some preference for the shiny ones. You're easier to find in a dark club that way."

She scowled and then told him, "I dress for the girls anyway. They're the only ones who appreciate the work that goes into being glamorous."

"Oh, I appreciate the result," Jack said. "I just don't care if your dress is black or blue."

While he teased her, he found her favorite kimonos and folded them carefully, adding in the pajamas she preferred to sleep in. She watched him with her own hovering smile while she hung her dresses at the top of her trunk. Before long, her bags were packed and she was curled up by his side.

"Where do you want to go?" she asked him as he tangled their fingers together, lifting her hand to press a kiss on each fingertip.

"I don't care," Jack replied easily.

"What you aren't going to say is it doesn't matter as long as we're together?" Vi asked.

Jack laughed and shrugged despite being propped up against pillows.

Vi turned, leaning up on her elbow. "You're in a good mood, Jack. I'd say…giddy even."

"Giddy?"

"As a school girl," she shot back.

He tugged her back down to him and said, "I suppose I'm excited about this trip too. Where do you want to go?"

"I don't care," she admitted. "Somewhere we haven't been before."

"Somewhere we haven't been before is perfect," Jack quickly agreed and she guessed that he'd be fine with Cuba, the Amalfi Coast, Rio de Janeiro, or even just their London house. She could say it for him, just as long as they were together.

CHAPTER 2

They reached the train station in early afternoon. Most of the steamships they'd consider taking wouldn't be leaving until after a goodbye party with the travelers and their guests. The evening party allowed them time to gather up their trunks and autos. Then, they could take a train to a port city.

The luxury liners were a vacation on their own. They had cruise directors with entertainment the whole day. On the last cruise they'd taken, Vi and Kate had attended a lecture from an Oxford professor about the flora and fauna of the Cuban island. There would also be shuffle-board and a gymnasium and evenings with dancing as jazz bands played with sultry singers.

Vi looked forward to the feasts served on the ship and the evening dancing. She loved that on a steamship you'd find people from all over the world and then learn little things about someone from Belgium or America or Mexico. It never mattered where they were from or why they were different. In America, they held their utensils differently. It was just random bits of information that added a layer of dimension to the country when she thought about those places.

"Where?" Vi asked when Ham and Jack approached their group. She was sitting on one of her trunks with several more stacked nearby. It was late enough in the afternoon and warm enough that she was glad to have skipped a coat. They were under the side of a building while Jack and Ham had visited several of the offices to see what was available.

"It occurs to me," Victor said suddenly before the others could answer, "how ridiculous we're being."

"Ridiculous or not—" Jack tilted his head and shrugged, "We've got options."

"The destinations with room for us are Ankaran, Slovenia…"

"Oh, I've heard good things about Ljubljana. We could stay on the shore for a few days and travel into the interior," Rita interjected. "I haven't been to Slovenia, but I'm sure it's lovely."

"I don't even know where that is," Lila yawned. "It sounds like something from one of Vi's weird Tarzan books."

"She says it as if she hasn't read them," Vi snuck in.

Lila smirked, but didn't reply as Denny asked, "Was that the only option? Does Slovenia sound fun? I don't know if it sounds fun. It sounds…like I don't know. I'm getting images of a…of a…for some reason I'm thinking of that vampire novel."

"It's the 'ya," Rita said. "Transylvania…Slovenia."

"Well, I feel like I might start eating bugs. I feel certain there are nightmares ahead." Denny shrugged. "What else is there?"

"It's different and exotic," Jack pointed out. "Isn't that what we were looking for?"

"Rio De Janeiro was an option." Ham stepped out of the way of a bypassing family with three shrieking children. The entire group paused and watched them head towards one of the boats. "That was Slovenia."

"Rio de Janeiro is different and exotic," Rita said, looking excited. "I've wanted to go there for so long."

"Perth, Australia," Jack finished, "was the final option for today if we want to spend the whole of the year traveling. These places take at least two months to get there and back."

"Perth," Vi and Victor said in unison.

"Two months, Vi," Jack added. "And that's if we only spend a short time actually there."

Vi shrugged and said, "Australia sounds like an adventure for certain. They have those marsupials with babies in their tummies or whatever they are."

"Rio," Rita offered. "They have beaches, casinos, night clubs, and it's the other side of the world." Her mouth twisted and she said, "But that is another few months. I... want to. But I'm not prepared to be quite so wild on a whim and without research. I suppose reality is settling in. I don't think Father should like it if we disappeared for months without notice."

They all looked at each other and Vi asked, "What about places that are closer that are also not Slovenia?"

"There's the Bahamas, the east coast of the United States, or Oslo, Norway."

"Do those ships have room for all of us?"

Jack and Ham nodded in unison. It seemed the two of them had already discussed the timing and come to the same conclusion. Neither were prepared for a trip that would last months without notice.

Together Vi and Rita eyed each other and said, "Norway."

"With a reservation for both Rio and Perth in the future," Vi added.

Rita nodded and then glanced at the others. There were no objections other than Denny who said, "Perhaps we're being too hasty on Slovenia."

"Says the bug eater," Victor snapped. "You just don't want to be blamed if we find out later Slovenia is wonderful and we should have gone there the whole time instead of Norway."

Denny nodded without regret and everyone but Lila groaned.

Vi scrunched her nose and said, "We could let the clock decide."

Jack shook his head. "With the parties before we leave, everyone will be leaving as the party ends and they send off those who aren't going. It won't be enough of a difference time wise, and we won't know until after it's too late."

Vi eyed Rita who eyed her back. Both of them were rather firm in their desires, and each of them wished to go somewhere farther away. They both knew that their husbands did not have the same desire. It had felt like a long-lived wish that she wanted to visit Australia the moment it was said. Rita had already mentioned Rio de Janeiro more than once and before the last few days. Vi's mouth twisted. No, it was much too far with Kate's baby on the way and the twins and baby Lily.

With two nannies, three babies, Vi, Jack, Ham, Rita, Victor,Kate, Denny and Lila they were quite the large crowd. Probably too large to easily find room on any ship without notice.

"It occurs to me," Rita said, glancing at their group, "that a last minute trip with no preparation means maybe we should just vote?"

"No," Victor disagreed, wrapping his arm around Kate's waist. "We need something more whimsical than that."

They turned away from each other as they tried to decide how to decide.

"I didn't expect so many places that Rita hadn't been," Vi admitted. "I blame you for having not traveled further. You should have been to Rio or Perth before now, let alone Norway and Slovenia. This is your fault."

Rita gasped and narrowed her gaze at Vi. "It's not my fault that I've been to the United States. Surely you have as well."

Vi shrugged. Perhaps, once.

"Let's just choose Norway," Ham said, "before we begin our trip with hair-pulling. Everyone but Denny is happy enough with Norway. There's a place there called North Cape that I've heard of before. I shouldn't mind seeing that."

Both Vi and Rita turned on Ham, who grinned evilly.

Lila asked silkily, "Hair pulling, my good man? Someone is feeling daring to say such a thing to a new wife.

"Let's choose where we're and start our trip," Rita said, elbowing Ham for both herself and Vi.

"Which won't ever be over until they have a new wardrobe," Denny muttered and glanced at Lila, who had been slimming down and was touchy about her clothes fitting and refused to buy more until she was at her previous shape. "How many shops will they drag us to, Jack? They've not an ounce of sympathy even when I run out of chocolate."

"We'll get her to buy something," Vi told Denny as if he'd been worried over that. His dark look said he hoped to avoid shopping this time around, the foolish man. There was a good reason, Vi thought, that Lila called him a lad.

Kate laughed and then hooked her arm through Lila's. "I'll shop for accessories with you, Lila."

"Even my feet are different. Most of my shoes have abandoned me," Lila groaned. "I suppose I could find a headpiece."

Vi laughed and then ducked when she got matching dark looks from Lila and Kate, who were far more alarming than the mildly irritated Ham. Vi's gaze moved away more out of self-defense than a desire to people-watch, but her gaze was caught by another group. There were five or six of them with fabulous clothes and shoes. Even their trunks were fabulous.

There were two younger women, near Vi's age. They were twins which caught Vi's attention as a twin herself. But these twins were identical. They both had long dark hair that curled fabulously. It wasn't the style, but it was absolutely the right choice for those perfect manes. Each of them wore slinky dresses. Each of them stood next to tall, smooth men. Of the men, one was a brunette with a golden edge to his hair, and the other was pure white blonde. Both gents looked expensive.

The next woman was a curly-haired, voluptuous blonde. Her dress wasn't quite so nice, but she giggled loudly and both men watched the blonde rather than their own sleek wives. Vi lifted a brow at that, offended for the women on their arms, and then glanced at Rita.

"Looks like a bit of drama over there," Rita said, having noted the same thing Vi had. "Speaking of hair pulling…"

"What drama?" Ham asked.

"As the woman interpreter," Victor started and all the ladies groaned, "let me help you. Our girls are offended for the wives."

"The what?" Denny asked and both Ham and Jack groaned next.

"The wives are being snubbed in favor of that… poorer friend." Victor cleared his throat and then shuffled when Kate eyed him askance.

"It's not the financial status," Violet snapped.

"It's the status of *not his wife,*" Kate added. "Those gents are lusting after another woman in front of their wives. Look at the way the one in the darker dress is clutching her husband's arm. She's practically begging him to pay her attention."

Victor held up his hands in surrender. "I would never."

Kate's low laugh relaxed him, though he glanced at his twin with a still-remaining panic in his gaze. Vi hid her smile. Poor Kate had been a little mad since she'd gotten pregnant with the twins and her body had gone crazy. She was the calmest of them all…when she was not pregnant.

"Let's go where they're going," Denny suggested suddenly. "They look like they'll be good fun when we're bored amongst ourselves."

"That feels like a bad idea," Ham said. "If they explode…we could get hit with the shrapnel."

"Relationship shrapnel isn't so dangerous for non-friends. And we'll get to watch," Denny added happily. "So much better than shuffleboard. It will only be for the steamship. We'll go dancing in Oslo or wherever without them."

Vi and Rita found everyone looking to them, so they looked at each other instead. Rita shrugged and Vi found herself doing the same.

"I suppose it would make it random. We have no idea where that group is going," Rita said easily. "And it's not like we can't go to the other place the next time we travel."

"What if…" Vi grinned and then suggested, "What if we just travel to one location—wherever they're going—and then try to find a ship from there to another place if we don't like it. There's no reason, really, why we can't get our own way."

Rita nodded immediately, and the two of them glanced at the rest of their group.

"I suppose we don't have a deadline," Jack said. "Even if a forty plus day trip seems a bit long without notice."

"The wonders of being unemployed," Ham muttered and only Jack winced with him.

The rest of them were happily unemployed while Ham and Jack were struggling with leaving behind Scotland

Yard for something else…anything else? They weren't sure, though they had begun to work with their private investigator…would they call Smith a friend? He was a friend, Vi decided. But he was the kind of friend who would go through your things, eat your Christmas pudding, and still somehow charm his way back for New Year's supper.

"Indeed," Vi said easily.

Ham had chosen for himself and in doing so, chosen for Jack who had never been quite a normal employee at the Yard. Without Ham, Jack had been told not to come back. She did feel bad that they were floundering, but she also felt that there was far more to them than Scotland Yard. Without the constraints? Maybe they'd be what they were always meant to be. Either way, the day was supposed to be about an exciting trip.

"We could gamble over it," Denny suggested as they hadn't fully decided yet.

"I'll be woebegone without both long-distance places now," Rita said, batting her lashes dramatically, until Denny groaned and Victor snickered into Kate's hair.

"She makes it sound as though she's Oliver Twist denied extra food," Ham told Jack dryly. "It's going to work too."

"Oh it worked. Find out where they're going," Jack said. "Rio and Perth. Here we come…"

"Eventually," Vi inserted and Jack grinned.

"Or…" Denny's mischievous giggle filled the air and had Jack and Ham groaning.

"Oh," Victor laughed, "I can see what you think." He laughed too.

"Are we telepathic now?" Lila asked. She glanced at

her husband who was staring at Jack and Ham and chuckling. "Oh…" She tilted her head and laughed lightly. "Denny wants you to sleuth out where they're going and then buy the tickets."

Ham rolled his eyes and glanced at Jack. "They're going to Norway."

"How can you tell?" Denny demanded.

"They're Norwegian."

"How can you tell?" Denny demanded.

Ham snorted and then Jack said, "We heard them speaking."

"Cheating!" Denny crowed. "Cheating!"

"Two of them are so blonde they make Irish people seem as though they have dark complexions. They also have that post-trip exhaustion. The second twin in the lighter blue dress with the run in her stockings looks ready to sag into her husband," Violet added.

"Perhaps they're Brits who have been living in Brazil for quite some time," Lila suggested, "assuming you hadn't heard them speak. Maybe they're taking that long trip to Rio and we're the fools who are going to Norway. Is it snowing in Norway right now?"

"That's also an option," Jack replied, unbothered by their teasing. He somehow didn't mind the frivolity of their little family despite being so much more serious than the rest of them. "But the pièce de résistance is, of course, the fact that the secretary or whoever she is, is holding a bag with a tag that has the Norwegian flag."

"Fine then," Denny said, not hiding his pout. "You really are investigators."

"Or," Ham said, "there is the fact that their things are

being loaded by one of the porters for the Annabelle, which is the ship sailing to Norway."

"They're working with information we don't have," Denny announced. "This is certainly cheating."

"They're working with skills you don't have," Kate said with a laugh, and then was distracted immediately when baby Agatha reached for her. Then, Vivi demanded to be held and lifted her arms for whoever would take her up. Denny picked her up and she squeezed his cheeks and then flopped her body towards Vi who caught her just in time.

"Ouch," Denny said, holding his chest. "Such attacks as these…being abandoned by Vivi…cruel. Too, too cruel." When no one agreed with him, he said, "So Oslo then? Sounds like a fellow I once knew." He pretended to introduce his friend and added, "Ozzy, my good man, meet my friends."

After a moment, Denny frowned and then said, "Is it winter in Norway?"

Vi's gaze widened at the question and then she said kindly, "Denny darling, of course, it isn't. Norway isn't Australia."

"But it is cold there, though, isn't it? Even in the summer?"

They all glanced at each other. After a moment, Vi demanded, "Who packed a coat?"

Only Rita and Kate raised their hands. Neither of the nannies had joined in, but Vi could tell from their controlled expressions that they had known they could have ended anywhere and were prepared. The good news was that meant the babies were prepared as well.

Vi shrugged and said, "It's Norway. It probably isn't

that cold during the summer even if it's quite a bit colder during the winter. Either way, it can't be so cold we won't survive until we acquire one."

"Winter in Rio," Rita said with a bit of a vow, "is the best time to go. We'll need to remember that for next year."

CHAPTER 3

They were led to their rooms with enough time to situate themselves, rest, and change for the dinner and party. Vi took one look at the room and flopped onto the bed, rolling onto her back.

"What do you think there is to do in Oslo?"

Jack took off his suit jacket and folded it over the back of a small chair before he replied, "Probably the exact same things we do in London but with different scenery."

Vi scowled at Jack and then couldn't help but grin, since she could see the smirk flirting about the edge of his mouth. She sighed and let her eyes close. Even though they were in port, the ship was rocking slightly and the smell of the sea in the air made it seem as though there were endless possibilities ahead.

"You like to visit new places," Vi said when Jack lay down next to her. "You can't fool me."

"I should like to go fishing in the ocean."

Vi scrunched her nose, but she didn't mind him seeking out his own adventures any more than he minded her. "Perhaps we could find some horses to ride on the beach. I do always enjoy a long horseback ride."

They traded ideas until a steward knocked on their door to remind them of the time and return to their evening clothes. Vi slowly sat up and stretched each leg out. Her head tilted and she asked, "What do we have to do for a tray of Turkish coffee?"

The gent grinned at her and said, "Nothing, ma'am. I'll have it to you soon."

When he left, Vi started putting on her cosmetics and underthings, almost tasting the coffee in her mouth. She wasn't sure she'd be lively without a coffee before they left for dinner and dancing. She glanced at Jack who had the wit to pack their own drinks, and he poured her a glass of ginger wine while they waited.

She slowly looked through her things, distracted from her cosmetics, and dug out stockings that went with her dress, her shoes, and her jewelry. Jack locked her remaining jewelry up and then smoothed back his hair while standing over her. She looked up from powdering her nose to see him run the comb through his hair, and she giggled into her puff.

"Oh, steamships," she said lightly. "Shall we just weave ourselves together now?"

"Spoilt," he muttered with a smirk that had been too apparent lately.

Vi examined his face in the mirror and wondered what was happening with him. She thought he might just be trying so hard to be happy about not working for Scotland Yard and finding his way through, that he'd slipped out of his natural state. Rather than worry too much about it, she decided to let it go for the moment. He'd find his new balance, and if he needed to pretend to be giddy along the way, she supposed she'd survive.

"Spoilt?" she returned lightly. "You're as used to dressing rooms and private baths as I am, sirrah."

"True," he said, dropping a kiss on her head before she started with her lipstick, "but I think we both know you're more spoiled than I."

"I will admit no such thing," she said.

They both paused when they heard someone outside their door. Then Jack opened it while Vi slipped behind the dressing screen and put the kimono over her head. While she did, Jack pulled in a coffee tray on a cart and said something low. As Vi stepped out from behind the screen, he handed her a cup of her Turkish coffee and she slumped back into the vanity chair with a satisfied sigh.

"Our steward has one of the twins across the way," Jack told her. "They ordered something or other as well. The one with the blonde gent."

Vi snorted. "Poor Denny. He probably has some retired schoolmarm across from him."

"Shall we swap rooms with them?" Jack asked.

Vi shook her head. She wasn't moving again. She'd made friends with the bed, such as it was, and until they left the ship, this bed was her ally. Besides, if it wasn't exciting across the hall, Denny would moan, and if it was exciting across the hall, Denny would never stop re-describing what he'd seen through the peep hole.

"Ready to go dancing?" Vi asked.

They'd been too late with their tickets to be assigned

the same table with the rest of their friends, but two couples would be able to sit together at each of the tables at a time, so the four couples had decided to switch up who sat with who each evening.

"Dining anyway," Jack agreed.

Vi gasped and reached up to take hold of his tie. "Dancing," she ordered fiercely.

He grinned slowly at her and then shrugged. He was still handsome, though his face was upside down and his humor didn't quite match his usual self. Her gaze narrowed on him and he shrugged again. "There's always watching the moon rise on the ocean. The stars will be bright if they aren't foiled by clouds."

Vi spun and stood, facing him as she took hold of his lapels, ensuring she had his full attention. "Do you not want to dance?"

His gaze searched hers and then he admitted, "Perhaps not all evening long."

"You'd rather watch the stars then?"

"I think we might even find one of those lounge style chairs, darling. We could watch them and think."

It was the 'and think' that made Vi grin and nod. She knew it meant that he wanted to ponder on his situation and perhaps on the cases he'd been considering with Smith. Jack wasn't so much considering taking on those cases as looking at what Smith worked on and debating the merits of spending his time following something similar.

If he needed some quiet by the rail of a ship, staring at the stars with her, she'd be there. She suddenly understood why Jack had suggested not going back to London. A whimsical trip to anywhere wasn't her Jack. It was

Rita, Victor, Vi, even Denny, but it wasn't Jack. However, avoiding London until they had a plan made sense to Violet.

"That sounds nice," Vi said, patting his chest. "I should like to see the stars without the murk of London or fighting through the trees."

They finished dressing and Vi finished a second cup of Turkish coffee before they started to hear other ship goers in the passageway. Vi's dress was an off-white sheath that reached from her shoulders to her feet. Over the top of the sheath, a sequined black lace covering exposed a bit of an Egyptian mermaid pattern in the contrast between the off-white and black.

Jack lit a cigar as they stepped into the passageway, finding one of the twins they'd been watching earlier leaving her room at just that moment.

"Oh hello," Vi said, grinning easily. She ignored the way the woman adjusted her shawl around her shoulders hiding an unfortunate bruise. Vi would have reacted, but it was so clear that the girl didn't want them to notice the bruise that Vi pretended. "Lovely day."

"Oh yes, hello," the twin stuttered. Vi was a little surprised the woman's accent was British when they'd been so convinced her husband had been Norwegian, but Vi kept her thoughts to herself. "Isn't it just though."

"Just visiting Norway?" Vi asked as they approached the same exit to the passage.

"Oh no—" The woman gave Vi and Jack a polite smile. "I live in Oslo now."

"Visiting home must have been fun," Vi said.

Another polite smile that didn't reach her eyes and Vi

guessed that nothing was very fun for this woman. Vi let her pass and then lingered back with Jack.

"Did you see?" Vi looked up at Jack and saw that his eyes weren't smiling or even pretending to smile anymore. He nodded once and then they both sighed. There was nothing to be done for someone who didn't ask for help. Even then, divorce was hard and messy and could ruin you.

Jack held out his arm and they entered the grand dining room with sickened stomachs. They gave their names and were seated at the same table as Victor and Kate. Then Vi noticed that the other twin and her husband were at the same table.

They introduced themselves to the others and got the name of the man and his wife. He was Oskar Nielsen and she was Ruth. Violet would have loved to know Ruth well enough to wonder whether her marriage were as seemingly unhappy as her sister's. Vi also wanted to know how both British sisters ended up in Norway.

Instead, Vi asked, "You're Norwegian, I think," to Mr. Nielsen who nodded in reply, accepting his cocktail from the waiter with delight.

"Indeed," Mr. Nielsen replied. "Born and bred." He laughed as though his joke were quite funny and Vi's friends echoed the laugh without the same eagerness.

Vi accepted her own cocktail, noting the limp mint and wishing her drink had been made by her twin. She noticed his unhappy expression after he sipped his own drink. "They're not very good with their drinks, are they?"

"I find the Annabelle to be generally not very good,"

Mr. Nielsen replied. "We've sailed on her many times, haven't we, darling?"

His wife gave an uninterested nod, but Mr. Nielsen didn't seem to mind or even notice. He glanced at her, saw the nod, and looked away. She sipped from her drink and then noticed Vi's pearls.

"How lovely they are," she said to Vi in a low voice as her husband caught the attention of Jack and Victor.

"Thank you," Vi said, almost rubbing her hands together with glee. "They were from my twin." Vi's glance led Mrs. Nielsen to Victor who grinned at her.

"Oh," Ruth Nielsen said, "I see it now. You are very similar, aren't you?"

They were the male and female halves of the same coin. With sharp features, active expressions, slim frames, and dark coloring, they definitely looked related.

"I'm a twin as well." Ruth Nielsen's dark brown eyes moved to her sister a table over. Vi noted Denny and Lila at that same table and then winked at him when he saw her attention.

Vi turned and glanced at the woman she'd spoken to outside of her cabin. "How fun is it to look just the same. We would have caused endless trouble with that."

"Oh we would have," Victor agreed merrily, setting his drink aside with another scowl. "Our poor step-mother would have yanked her hair out of her head in sheer frustration."

Violet and Victor grinned at each other, not needing to interpret the other's thoughts. Possibilities were unfolding between them as they considered the idea. It ended with identical evil smirks and they glanced in unison at Ruth Nielsen.

She chuckled low. "You *are* twins, aren't you. I feel like Margaret and I have read each other's minds since before I can remember."

"Does your sister live in Norway as well?"

"Oh yes," Ruth grinned. "She moved with me when I married Oskar. It wasn't very long before Liam and Margaret married. She's Mrs. Hanson now."

Vi examined Ruth's face for any emotion about that statement, but there wasn't anything to see. Vi tried to hide her own thoughts and watched as Jack idly chatted with Oskar Nielsen. Vi wouldn't be surprised if Jack had discovered far more information from Oskar without even trying, than Vi had. All she'd discovered was names to go with the guesses they'd already made. Vi's mouth twisted and she tried her cocktail again to her immediate regret.

CHAPTER 4

The dinner was fine without being good and Vi thought back to her Turkish coffee, instantly grateful that it, at least, had been quite good. When dinner ended, Vi and Jack slipped out of the dining room as did the rest of the guests. It was being converted from a dining room to a ballroom and guests of the departing seafarers were able to join for the evening just before the ship departed.

They found Lila and Denny near the end of the ship gazing at the arriving guests. People were dressed almost as luxuriously here as for a night at the opera and there was an air of frivolity. Vi sidled up to Denny and asked, "Did you see the bruise?"

"Oh, I saw it. Did you get a good look?"

Vi shook her head. "Was her husband awful?"

Vi paused when she caught sight of one of the twins, but it took a moment to realize it wasn't a twin at all, but was Oskar Nielsen and the curvy little blonde who had boarded the ship with them. They were in the shadows of a doorway, and Vi elbowed Denny and jerked her head when she realized that the couple was kissing fervently.

"Oh bloody hell," Denny breathed, shaking his head. "Anyone could see them out there."

"He isn't even the violent one," Vi said. "Doesn't seem like either of the women are happy in their marriages."

"Did you *see* the bruise, Vi? You could see each finger of the fellow on her shoulder. It made me sick. Felt the need to apologize to Lila even though she'd murder me rather than put up with that nonsense."

"You'd get arsenic chocolates for certain," Vi told Denny easily.

"It would be my duty as a mother," Lila told Denny dryly. "Allowing myself to be abused in front of Lily would make her feel like it was just how things were. I won't have that."

Vi blinked a little rapidly. Anything serious from Lila was so rare, Vi was almost surprised.

"I would rather you protect Lily than me," Denny said, patting her hand on his arm.

Vi laughed and glanced at the others.

"Did Denny just give Lila permission to murder him?" Victor cleared his throat to hide his laugh.

"For Lily's sake." Denny shrugged. "What wouldn't we do for our daughters?"

Kate squeezed Victor's arm. "I don't have to worry about Victor. He was trained by Vi long before I came along."

Vi snorted and giggled at the same time and had to steal Jack's handkerchief to collect herself. As soon as she was recovered, she pushed up on her toes to see if Oskar

Nielsen and not-his-wife were still in the passageway, but they had disappeared.

"They went down to the cabins," Jack told Vi. His tone told her what he thought they were going to do and how he felt about disappearing on a wife with another woman.

"They could try a little harder to hide things," Lila muttered. "Any woman with half a wit would notice them disappearing and coming back rumpled."

"Maybe she doesn't care," Kate suggested.

A moment later Rita and Ham appeared in the passageway. "Guess what we saw?"

"The blonder of the gents we followed onto the ship," Jack said quickly. "With the not-his-wife disappearing towards the cabins?"

Rita glanced at Ham and slowly shook her head. "The twin with the bruises and another fellow. Not-her-husband…"

Vi gasped and then said, "I wonder if that's why she has the bruises. Did you see them too?"

"A shawl isn't a very good disguise," Ham said. "We saw them when we were leaving the dining room."

"Who is the fellow she was with in the hallway?" Vi asked, glancing at Jack. She saw the smirk on his face and said, "Yes, we're incurably nosy."

"Maybe she has a lover," Rita suggested. She hesitated long enough that Vi waited for an expansion of her thoughts, but Rita just scrunched her nose and shrugged.

"Did they not look like lovers?" Vi asked.

"They were awfully close together," Ham added, but he shook his head too. "Far closer than strangers would ever be."

"Maybe they were just conspiring about something," Vi said, given that they'd both paused. "Maybe she owes the fellow money or knows something about him."

"Maybe they're friends," Victor added. "We are all rather comfortable with each other."

"Then why were they hiding in the shadows?" Ham asked. He shook his head and said, "I'm not sure why I'm thinking about this. I don't even care."

Jack snorted and Vi elbowed him lightly.

"So who is the bruiser of Margaret?" Denny asked with too much relish. He got a dirty look from every woman around him and winced, but his interest was peaked, and he couldn't hide it. "I'm not happy she's bruised." There was a bit of a whine in his voice. "I'm just interested in why."

"The most likely person to hurt a woman is the person you would tell yourself wouldn't." Ham looked disgusted and he glanced down at Rita with an expression that was unreadable. It was, however, guessable given the conversation. Vi bet Ham was incapable of even imagining hurting Rita. That's what made Ham and Jack and Victor and Denny the men that they were.

"You mean her husband?" Lila asked. "I'm not surprised. Most of the women I know who've been hurt have been hurt by a husband, father, or brother. Men as a rule are rather undesirable risks."

"Their fathers?" Denny gasped and then shook his head, rejecting the idea vigorously.

"Surely we know far more men," Rita countered, "who wouldn't leave their wife bruised and hurt."

"Let alone *fathers*," Denny said fiercely. Vi was almost surprised, but there was more to Denny than giggles and chocolate even if he rarely showed those parts of himself.

"So," Vi added easily, hoping to lighten the mood, "you're saying that more men are good than bad?"

"Yes," Denny muttered and then gasped dramatically when the bruised twin's husband appeared. He whispered loudly, "What's his name?"

"Liam Hanson," Jack replied low.

The fellow was looking for someone. He was standing tall and straight scanning the crowd. Was he looking for his wife? Would he be enraged when he found her? Would there be more bruises?

Maybe he wasn't even looking for his wife. Maybe... "What if he's looking for the curvy blonde?"

Denny gasped and said, "Vi! You have a diabolical mind."

She grinned evilly at him, and he matched her. The others groaned a bit and Rita said, "I feel certain this steamship journey will end with us knowing far too much about those twins, their lovers, their husbands, and their details."

Vi gasped, but she was already plotting how to get more information. An idea occurred to her and she glanced at Jack. A moment later she shook her head.

"What?"

Her answer was to tell Denny, "Ask the twins to dance."

"And the curvy blonde," Lila added. "Flirt with her and see if she responds."

"It really should be Victor as well. He could play the twin angle, he's clearly expensive..."

"I'm what?" Victor gasped.

"You're like a fine wine," Rita told him. "Expensive and pretty."

His mouth dropped and he looked to his wife for assurance, but she was too busy laughing to comfort him.

"Denny is too much like a puppy for not-his-wife if she's looking to upgrade from lover to wife." Lila glanced at him with consideration. "You should ask the bruised one to dance. You aren't alarming and she might be nervous of men."

"I could be alarming," Denny said with a frown. He paused and then laughed. "Perhaps not."

"Perhaps not," Vi agreed in unison with Lila. They laughed and then Kate said, "It's not a bad thing to be someone safe."

"You're so nice," Rita told Kate. To Victor, Rita said, "She's so nice."

"She is. She made the puppy feel better," Victor said, sliding his arm around his wife's waist.

"At least I'm not pretty and expensive," Denny muttered. "Victor sounds like a courtesan."

Vi gasped, choking on a laugh. She turned to hide her giggles in Jack's arm.

"It does sound like a courtesan," Ham told Victor. "Sorry, old man."

"Oh thank you," Victor said wryly. "I so appreciate your concern."

Vi glanced at Jack. "We're going to go for a walk before we dance."

The others nodded and Victor said, "I'll be visiting the bar and making my own drink."

Vi grinned at her twin and then let Jack tug her away. They could hear the sound of stringed instruments tuning, and the lights of the dining room were shining out onto the walkway around the ship. The guests began to move back into the dining room that had been transformed into a ballroom.

"Jack," Vi said carefully when they found themselves alone. "Are you all right?"

"I'm fine," Jack said.

"You are not," Vi countered. "I can tell that you're not feeling yourself."

He wound their fingers together and pressed a kiss on her forehead. "Perhaps I am not. Perhaps I even have a touch of the grey days, but not entirely, Vi. I *am* happy. I would choose this life with you over any other possibility."

Vi searched his gaze and then pushed up on her toes, taking his face in her hands. "I just want you to be happy."

"And I just want *you* to be happy."

Vi lifted a brow and then wrapped her arms around his waist, leaning against his chest. "I suppose I know all about grey days. It's possible to know you are blessed and still wish things were different."

"I don't even feel unhappy, Vi. It's not that. I feel unanchored."

Vi didn't blame him. She'd felt that way when her great aunt died. She'd felt like that when she realized she was running Aunt Agatha's businesses. She'd felt like that time and again as she and Victor had been tugged apart by their own lives.

Even now, she missed her twin desperately. He was aboard ship with them, and at dinner, they'd share coffee and talk about books, but a part of her just wanted to revisit the days when they'd shared rooms and lived in each other's pockets.

Vi squeezed Jack's hand and took a deep breath.

"Shall we dig into those twins' lives?"

"I'd rather not," Jack admitted.

Vi laughed. "But I only packed a dozen books."

Jack rubbed his chin over the top of her head and suggested, "Perhaps write one with Victor then."

Vi narrowed her gaze on Jack and then she turned to face the sea. They were still in the London port, which was always busy. If you paid attention, the sound of the shore, the sound of water traffic, the lull of the waves all contributed to a sort of busy, appealing song.

"What if we purchased a yacht?" Vi asked when they saw a luxurious one in the distance.

"Do we enjoy sailing?" Jack asked. "Wouldn't you rather have a place by the sea?"

Vi considered, "Perhaps in Lyme?"

"Or Southwold?"

"Ooh," Vi agreed immediately.

She was leaning into Jack when Liam Hanson appeared. He wasn't looking for anyone anymore, but was leaning over the railing smoking a cigarette. If he'd found who he'd been looking for, there was no sign.

Vi shivered and Jack warmed her by placing his suit jacket around her shoulders. She felt the weight of Jack's hands on her shoulders, and a part of her imagined Jack digging his fingers into her body like that. She knew he never would, but what if he *did*?

How heartbreaking would it be to have Jack betray her trust like that? She wondered, if Mr. Hanson were the one who hurt his wife, did he apologize? Did he just assume it was his wife's due? Maybe, if it started before they were married, he apologized then? Vi wished she could take aside Mrs. Hanson, demand a name of who was hurting her, and then convince the woman she had options beyond just accepting what was happening.

"Thank you for being you," Violet told Jack with her gaze on Mr. Hanson.

"Mmm," Jack said, seeming to understand the nature of her thoughts. "Why don't we dance until the ship leaves and then find a place to watch the stars?"

Vi was sold on the idea before he had finished saying it.

CHAPTER 5

$\mathcal{V}$i had spent some time on a steamship or two. It wasn't all that shocking to walk into a ballroom and be awed. The Annabelle, however, did not inspire awe. She'd been in there earlier for dinner and hadn't been expecting a miracle, but if anything, she was a little surprised it was so poorly done.

The four-piece quartet was pushed into a corner. There wasn't a singer and the music was more 1820s style than 1920s style. Vi heard a country dance and saw the guests on the ship trying and failing to make it through the steps.

Vi giggled into her hand when Denny crashed into Ham and then the two of them brushed each other off. They seemed to be having a good time despite everything. Denny took Ham in his arms and danced him around their wives in what looked more like a drunken gallop than any sort of choreographed dance.

"Our friends are idiots," Jack told her. He pulled her

into his arms and over to their friends, crashing into Denny on purpose. He turned at the last moment so Vi wasn't included in the crash.

"Hullo," Denny said, catching Vi when she escaped the tangle. "Hullo, Hullo, there. Shall I save you from this brute?"

"I thought you were going to slide into Margaret Hanson's life and see if you could save her from her brute?"

Denny leaned in and then stage whispered, "She's not here."

Vi glanced around the floor noting her brother at the bar with his wife nearby. Neither of the twins, their husbands, or the curvy little blond were in attendance. Vi stepped back and as a group they shuffled to the side of the dance floor. There wasn't any sort of guidelines for what was considered dance floor and what wasn't, so there were couples attempting to dance near them while another group of people were chatting a few feet away, drinks in hand.

"Wherever are they?" Vi asked.

"There's nowhere else to go," Ham announced. "Rita and I have been looking into it. There's a particularly anemic little library, a smoking room for the gents that's too small and quite close, and a gymnasium. No ladies allowed."

Vi lifted a brow. She paused and then giggled into her hand until Rita demanded, "Why are you laughing?"

"This is what comes of buying tickets on the first ship available. The food isn't very good, the drinks are intolerable, the dancing is out-of-time, and there's nothing much to do but walk, sit, and entertain ourselves."

"We could get the musicians to at least play waltzes," Lila said. "Waltzing is romantic with the right man, isn't it? Better than this drivel."

Violet glanced at Jack, but he'd already started towards the players. She watched as he leaned into speaking with the cellist and then handed over some money. The music shifted from old style country dances to a waltz.

Violet spun towards Jack who held out his hand as he approached, and then they swung into the music. It was lovely to have his arm around her waist and their hands clasped. Vi looked at where their hands held each other and found herself waxing romantic at the sight of her hand, gloved in a long black silk, and the diamond bracelets on her wrist.

Violet and Jack spun round the room with controlled energy in perfect rhythm. She trusted him to lead, and it seemed that the happy dancing of Vi's party had extended to the others in the room. Vi noticed Victor's face in the twirling throng and then Lila's and Kate's. She saw Ham's face and the back of Rita's head, and then she saw Denny, but the short blond bob of Lila wasn't who he was dancing with. Vi's gaze widened, and she turned from Jack, leaving herself in his care, and noticed that Denny was dancing with Ruth Nielsen.

Vi smiled when she met the other woman's gaze, and then turned and found it was Victor, the "pretty and expensive," dancing with the curvy little blonde. He had a perfectly attentive smile on his face, which Vi knew meant he was bored or upset. It was his mask and he had worn it often before he married Kate.

"Poor Victor," Vi told Jack, who followed her gaze and then moved them towards her brother.

When they came upon the other couple, Jack asked with a twinkle in his eye, "Might I cut in?"

Vi almost dropped her jaw, but the curvy little blonde glanced between Jack and Victor who were, clearly, equally expensive. The difference was Vi. Kate was a simple woman who wore light jewelry and plainer dresses. Vi liked sparkling things and expensive fashions. The little woman took in Vi's diamonds with complete and lascivious interest.

Jack swung the woman away and Vi told Victor, "He's a good egg."

"He's bent to your will. I'm sure he couldn't care less about the details of that woman's life."

"There's nothing else to do," Vi told him.

Victor held out his hand elegantly and Vi put hers in her twins. "Hello my dear brother."

"Hello my pretty devil," he replied. He danced them towards the bar and when he reached it, he placed a pound note on the bar and stepped behind it to make a drink for himself and Vi.

They leaned against the wall and watched Jack charm the pretty woman.

"What's her name?"

"Milly Kristiansen. She's the daughter of one of the partners. The two gents who married the twins are in business together with her father."

"But she seems so much less…"

"She's a widow," Victor told his twin with a proud smile that declared he knew that he'd delved into the woman's life rather quickly for a waltz.

"Is she?" Vi's tone was pure challenge.

"That's all I know," he admitted with a laugh.

Vi grinned and sipped her drink, then frowned at her brother.

"I'm afraid I can only make swill tolerable, darling. The barman isn't so unskilled. He's just got nothing but waste water to work with. Darling, we'll have to shop rather fiercely in Norway to see ourselves set right."

"Perhaps you can have a trunk made," Vi suggested. "Something like a mobile bar where you can travel with your own things."

"Yes," Victor said immediately. "Bloody hell, Vi. A brilliant aside, but perfect for Carlyle Spirits and Wines. I need to find a…a…luggage maker and then we'll collaborate on a design of my own." He frowned, sipped his drink, gagged a little, and nodded firmly. "Yes, of course."

Vi sipped and watched her husband charm the widow who had been traveling with her father's partners. Why was she traveling with them? Had she been sent to England to do some errand? She didn't have fresh enough gowns to have gone for a new wardrobe. Perhaps she'd gone to visit some friend and her father sent her along with his partners to have her looked after.

Violet scrunched her nose at the idea. A widowed woman having to travel with company. It was ridiculous to assume that she would be somehow unable to look after herself. Perhaps it was more…earthy…than that. Perhaps she had found the wisp of an excuse to go along simply so she could chase after her lover. Or was it lovers?

Violet leaned her head on Victor's arm and said, "I find myself thinking the most sensational thoughts. I think I could write French novels based upon my guesses about those twins, their husbands, and the partner's daughter."

"The sensational Mrs. Kristiansen." Victor snorted. "I suppose we could stop writing about ingenues and their adventures with storms and disturbing noises in the darkness and possible spectres, and write about loose women instead."

Vi scrunched her nose and said, "It's going to be a boring journey, but I suppose we'll survive."

"I suppose so," Victor agreed. "Shall we write a book?"

"That's what Jack suggested."

They considered each other and then noticed Lila, Denny, and Ruth Nielsen chatting together.

"Denny," they said in unison.

"He'll never let it go in favor of a novel," Victor added. "I suppose we could help him and then spend the rest of our trip sitting by the water."

Violet took a deep breath and whispered her confession. "I suppose I want to learn more about them too. People are such interesting creatures, aren't they?"

As though saying that they were interesting was a reasonable way to explain that she was incurably nosy, an unrepentant meddler, and that she was somehow a person who kept to her own devices like she was drawn into her nosiness against her will.

"They are indeed," Victor agreed with a humor that said he'd caught her fake excuses and was as amused by them as she was. He elbowed her slightly and Vi's gaze turned. Mr. and Mrs. Liam Hanson had entered the room. They were arm in arm, and the shawl had been pinned into place. There was a tightness to Margaret Hanson's mouth, and her gaze was cool and hard.

Were her eyes so cold because of whatever she had been doing? Or were they hard because her husband had *taken her in hand* once again? Vi reminded herself that she wasn't *certain* that it had been the husband who had bruised Margaret, though it did seem rather likely.

"I do want to know what's happening with those twins," Victor said low. "I suppose it's because they're twins. It's not like Margaret Hanson is the first wife I've seen treated poorly. What would I do if it were you? How can Ruth see whatever is happening and not react?"

"We don't know that she hasn't," Violet said. "She may have begged her sister time and again to leave her husband. Perhaps offered a refuge in her own home."

"This is where being male and female twins is different. Obviously we aren't referring to Jack here, but suppose your husband treated you that way? I'd murder him slowly and viciously."

Vi grinned at her brother and admitted, "I suppose, dear Victor, that you should know that I would do the same for you—man or not."

Violet laughed at the look on his face and then elbowed him. A man approached the married couple and spoke to them. Whatever he said had Mr. Hanson's face turning a ruddy furious red. Vi gasped and then watched as Margaret tried to calm both of the men down. She had a placating hand out and her husband snatched her wrist. Violet could tell from her vantage point that the fingers were digging in harshly.

Her brother had straightened and handed Vi his glass. She could see the growing anger on his face and knew he intended to help Margaret Hanson when her sister slipped in between the two with what looked like a casual aside.

In the process, however, Ruth had broken Liam Hanson's grip on her twin and when the adjusting of the little grouping had finished, Margaret was just behind her sister's shoulder, Ruth protecting her like a lazy angel.

She said something else, and the dark-haired gent flushed. He shot a comment back at Ruth and, clearly Margaret, and then stepped away, shooting furious glances over his shoulder.

Ruth laughed and then she said something else. It wasn't nearly so lazy because Vi could see Ruth's pretty face focused intently on her brother-in-law. Her hand was still on her twin, behind her back, and when she finished her comment, Liam Hanson stepped away.

Vi wanted desperately to eavesdrop on what the twins said to each other. They spoke in what looked like soft half-sentences that reminded Vi of how she and Victor could speak almost without words.

"What a—" Victor didn't finish.

"Yes." Vi glanced at him and then noticed the sisters walking away arm-in-arm. "I suppose we've discovered the bruiser, that Ruth is more involved than we realized, and that there is another party we didn't know of before."

"Who is he?" Victor asked.

"Who is he to Margaret?" Violet finished.

"And what will her husband do about it?"

CHAPTER 6

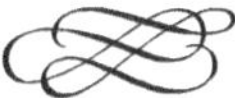

$\mathcal{V}$i had spent the rest of the evening drinking the barely tolerable drinks her brother made and chatting with him. When the twins and their husbands had disappeared, Jack and Ham had followed. Vi had seen the pacing lions in the men and knew the twins would be as safe as they could be.

They hadn't returned to the ballroom, but Vi wasn't concerned. This was no party worth lingering in, and she was enjoying the time with Victor. Rita had slipped out, found them smoking cigars near one of the railings, and Victor left them to dance.

"Is Ham struggling as much as Jack?" Vi asked when Victor swung Kate into another dance.

Rita glanced at Vi, her expression deepening with a stark guilt. Their gazes met and Rita nodded lightly.

"I don't know what to do about it," Vi admitted. "He said he feels unanchored."

"Ham doesn't say anything at all," Rita muttered. "I

can just tell. When we were talking about traveling anywhere, you could see that he wasn't comfortable with the idea of just…just…getting aboard a ship and leaving forever."

"Do you think that we're especially spoiled?" Vi asked.

Rita laughed until she cried, holding her stomach. "Most of England is spoiled compared to some of the places I've been. And us? Darling, we're the most spoiled of all."

"I suppose we are," Vi admitted.

She took a seat nearby and handed Rita the rather terrible cocktail. Rita took a sip, shuddered, but took another sip anyway. "This was supposed to be so fun."

Vi glanced at Rita and admitted, "I suspect we'd be less concerned with those twins and their husbands if the women were less beautiful and there was more to entertain us than watching people come and go."

Rita snorted, sipped, shuddered again, and then said clearly, "I didn't ask Ham to leave Scotland Yard."

Vi thought about that. Why *had* Ham left? "Could it have been your father?"

"Perhaps, in part." Rita wasn't as breezy as usual as she admitted it. "I don't know why. He might say Father had talked to him. But, Ham isn't a man who does things because another man tells him to. Even Jack listens to Ham."

"Perhaps things weren't as comfortable at Scotland Yard for him when we came along and interfered in his life as we have."

Vi's Jack had never fully been employed by Scotland Yard and his unique circumstances had been due to Ham. Their relationship existed long before the Yard. It went all the way back to the Great War when Ham ran investigations in the military. They'd been fighting for the survival of their way of life and what made them…them. Ham and Jack hadn't been able to fight the usual way.

Instead, they'd been sucked into investigative cases among their own people. Soldiers who'd died that shouldn't have. Missing munitions, blackmail and nefariousness among soldiers who had turned their attention from survival to something else. Something darker. And Ham and Jack and their fellows had stepped in and attempted to set things aright when they could never, actually, be right. The burden of their fight during the war had followed them home as much as their strong friendship.

"What are we supposed to do?" Rita asked.

Vi shook her head and said, "I suspect we should give them time and support them and wait until they find their balance again. It is what Jack has always done for me."

"But," Rita's mouth twisted, "I feel both guilty and afraid."

"Why are you afraid?" Vi asked softly.

Her brother was heading back this way, and she shot him a telling look. He took it in, winked at her, and tugged his wife from the ballroom.

Rita sighed. "Not everyone finds their balance, Vi. What if they don't?"

Vi winced at the idea and hoped they would be luckier than that. She fiddled with her wedding ring and said, "I suspect that we just have to have faith in them."

Rita linked their arms and rose when one of the stewards shot them a dark look that demanded they exit the ballroom so he could finish his work and get to bed. "I should like to be more active than that."

Violet glanced at the dingy sometimes-ballroom, sometimes-dining room and sighed. Rather than continuing to discuss their gents, Vi said, "I suppose we cannot judge Norway upon the Annabelle."

"No," Rita laughed. "Thought we might consider traveling home another way. This ship is…rather awful, isn't it?"

They left and found Ham and Jack only steps away. It was just like them, Vi thought, to linger nearby. Neither of them seemed tense or unanchored at that moment and Vi smiled gently at her husband. They hadn't been married all that long. They had only known each other since just before her great aunt's death and yet he'd become everything to her.

Violet leaned her head against Jack's shoulder. "This was the better way to spend this party."

"The guests are all gone. We'll be leaving soon."

"Shall we watch the world change?" Ham asked. His wife was under his arm, and he stared down at her almost in surprise. They'd been in love, they'd been broken apart, they were in love once again, married, but their happy ever after would never be as easy as Vi and Jack's.

"Let's," Rita said easily. They wandered towards the full length lounge chairs and curled into them side-by-side with Ham and Rita in one and Jack and Violet in another.

Within the hour, the ship started to move and they sat in silence. The chug of the ship's engines and the sound of the occasional person passing by invaded their quiet.

After a while, Ham rose and lifted the sleeping Rita in his arms.

"We're off," he said low, and Jack and Vi's only reply was a lifted hand.

Violet pressed her head back against Jack's chest and turned to face him. "This ship is terrible."

At the last moment, Violet bypassed asking Jack another question about his state of mind. She met his gaze, and she saw that he knew she was holding back. He pressed a kiss on her forehead and said, "It's not so bad. It's not a cattle car."

"I think I'd almost prefer some squished coach seating that is honest in what it is. This…this…Annabelle pretends to be quite luxurious and fails to deliver."

"Do we need to know how spoiled you are, darling Vi?"

"Rita has already lectured me on the subject. Did the twins get back to their rooms all right?"

"They're as safe as we could make them. I told the steward to keep out an ear and paid the fellow to interfere."

Vi's mouth twisted and she said, "I wish it were easier for a woman like Margaret Hanson to leave her husband when he hurts her."

Jack sighed and Violet placed her hands under her chin, propping up her head a little on Jack's chest.

"It is as easy as her family makes it," Jack told Violet. "Friends and family are what you need in times such as these are for Mrs. Hanson."

Violet thought of Ruth Nielsen who seemed almost disconnected from the world around her. Did she know her husband was cheating on her? Did she care? She realized, of course, that her twin was being abused, because she'd interfered that evening. But why hadn't they offered Margaret a home? Why hadn't Ruth done something more for her twin?

But why didn't Margaret do something for herself? Vi tried to imagine Jack hurting her and her leaving, but she couldn't do it.

"Maybe because they're business partners," Jack suggested. "It limits what Oskar Nielsen is willing to do."

Violet turned onto her side and then glanced up at the stars. The stars didn't move despite Jack and Violet moving. The stars, so far away, gave Vi and Jack the illusion of being still even though they could feel the rocking of the boat and the slow movement against the water. Vi's gaze moved from star-to-star. She knew the constellations, but she didn't care at the moment. She cared only that they were beautiful.

"Is there some way to help Margaret? Should we just ask her to her face?" Vi pretended to do just that. "Hello, we've noticed you're somewhat abused, and we'd like to offer you transportation to a safer place."

"She'd have to leave behind her sister, Vi. Perhaps, Ruth doesn't want to also leave her husband."

"Perhaps they can't afford themselves," Vi added. "Perhaps, they're concerned about a roof over their heads and food to eat. I suppose when describing being spoiled, there is me, who would be able to eat and live with or without you."

"Perhaps," Jack said. "There are endless perhaps, Violet. And you can't fix everyone's life."

Vi felt as though it were a message for himself rather than Margaret. Vi couldn't fix things for Jack or for

Margaret. But there was a second part to that as well. Each of them needed to change things for themselves.

She tangled their fingers together and placed her head against his chest, listening to his heartbeat. Her happiness had never been fixed by him, but his presence had helped her while she struggled through grey days and a blue outlook.

What had changed things for Vi was staying active, working on things she loves, spending time with her family, and ensuring she was sleeping and eating well enough. How simple it seemed, yet endlessly hard to accomplish.

Violet sighed and felt the creeping chill from the summer evening that even Jack couldn't fix in the face of winds off the water. She pushed up into a sitting position and said, "I'm going to go back to the room."

Jack hesitated and she pressed a kiss against his cheek. "Just me is fine, darling. I should like very much to take off this fabulous gown and put on my even-more-fabulous pajamas and a kimono. These cosmetics would do well on a washcloth rather than my face also."

Violet rose and made her way through the ship, almost missing her passageway and then her cabin. As she opened the door to the cabin she heard a loud noise in the cabin opposite. Vi's stomach dropped and her gaze widened when the steward slipped out of his little closet where he was at the ready for the first-class passengers. His gaze met hers as they heard the sound of flesh hitting flesh.

"I'll take care of it, Mrs. Wakefield." His name tag read M. Baldwin, and he knocked firmly on the door to the cabin, jiggling the handle when it wasn't opened.

Violet couldn't quite shut the door to her cabin. She left it cracked and listened as the steward pounded on the door. A drunk Liam Hanson answered the door, and whatever the steward said had Hanson growling at him.

Baldwin replied firmly and Hanson growled louder, pushing out into the passageway.

"If you think you can tell me how to treat my wife," Hanson snapped, "I'll teach you otherwise."

"Mr. Hanson." The steward's even tone was entirely without an emotional inflection. "You will leave this cabin and not return until the alcohol has left you, or you will find yourself in the brig until you've sobered up."

Mr. Hanson shoved past the steward, making him stumble hard into Violet's cracked cabin door. The poor man fell back, tripping over the lip of the cabin door and landing harshly on his back.

"Oh!" Vi said, kneeling down. "Are you all right?"

"Fine, fine," the steward said, but there was pain in his voice.

Violet helped him back up when he started to rise on his own, at the same time as Margaret Hanson found her way out of her cabin and offered her hand as well.

"He didn't know. He's…not aware of how harsh he is when he's in his cups."

Violet examined Margaret's face and asked softly, "Do you really believe that?"

Margaret didn't answer, but Vi could see that the woman did not believe her own lies. Violet moved to the case where Jack had pulled bourbon and ginger wine from earlier and poured both the steward and Margaret a drink.

She unapologetically handed both Margaret and the

steward aspirin and then told Margaret, "I suppose you know how to handle your bruises."

Margaret's face paled, but she didn't counteract the statement. To the steward, Vi said, "And I suppose you cannot take time to rest."

"The end of my shift is coming soon, Mrs. Wakefield."

Violet nodded and said, "Send both of our rooms Turkish coffee in the morning, would you?"

"That'll be Pederson on then, but I'll be sure he knows."

Violet nodded and then glanced at Margaret, who was staring towards her own cabin, apparently wanting to leave, but too hesitant to do so.

Gently, Violet said, "We'll all feel better in the morning."

"Of course," Margaret agreed, but neither of them believed it.

Violet said gently, "If you need help leaving him—"

"Thank you. No." Margaret shook her head and laughed bitterly. "No. I've nowhere to go."

"Your family won't help you?"

"My British family will never let a divorcee come home. Ruth would, but Oskar…there's nowhere."

"Perhaps that can be changed with a little thought and effort," Violet suggested.

"Believe me," Margaret told Violet starkly, "I'm far past a little thought and everything I have to give."

She left and Vi's gaze met Baldwin's. Both of them looked after Mrs. Hanson with terrible sympathy.

CHAPTER 7

Violet woke to the sound of a soft knock and she rose, put on her kimono, and crossed to the door quickly before Jack woke. They had stayed up far too late, approaching a full twenty-four hours awake by the time Jack had wrapped his arm around her waist.

She opened the door to the cabin and found Pederson, the morning steward, with two rolling carts. Vi took hers, carefully bringing the cart into the room as silently as possible. While she carefully maneuvered, Pederson knocked on the door opposite.

Vi admitted to herself that she was going a little more slowly when she realized she might get a glimpse of Margaret. The woman didn't, however, answer the door. Vi frowned and asked Pederson, "Did her husband come back?"

The fellow eyed her askance and asked, "You were the one who witnessed yesterday's kerfuffle?"

Vi nodded. "Just a little worried about her. Perhaps we should have the ship's doctor attend her?"

Pederson scowled and admitted, "I wouldn't see the ship's doctor unless I had no other choice, madam. If she's bruised, she'd be better off taking aspirin and a long rest."

Vi's gazed widened and she glanced down, only noting then the snagged carpets that were lining the hallway. This ship really was the worst. She thought that a little more time in research and a little less time in frivolity would have made for a far better trip.

Violet waited with Pederson and there was no answer.

"Should we check on her?" Vi asked. She wanted to, but she didn't have a key like Pederson.

He hesitated, placing a brake on the cart so that it could linger outside the room. He said, "We'll ask again in an hour."

Violet nodded and then slipped back into her cabin and into the tiny bathroom with a cup of Turkish coffee. There was quite a small bath and Violet stepped into it to wash off the day before. The water was barely warm, and she regretted the trip more and more.

"Norway will be lovely, my girl," she told herself with a faint hope. She had little doubt it would be lovely. In Norway, if their hotel was as undesirable as this hotel, they'd simply change hotels or even cities.

She was in no hurry because she didn't want to wake Jack, so she lingered in the bath until both the water and the coffee were cold and then she exited, in fresh pajamas and considered curling up next to Jack. She freshened her coffee and then risked cracking the door to see if

Margaret had taken her own coffee. The cart was missing, and Vi considered that a good sign, as the woman was able to get up and get her coffee.

Vi made her coffee and turned, finding Jack's gaze on hers. She crossed to him, handed him her cup and returned to make another for herself. She curled up next to him and said, "There was a ruckus last night. Mr. Baldwin, our steward, made Mr. Hanson leave."

Jack's jaw flexed and Vi said, "I was fine. Mr. Baldwin took a tumble."

Vi could see the rush of fury in Jack's gaze and knew that his protective instincts were high.

She repeated, "I was fine. I don't know that the same could be said for Margaret. I offered her help in leaving and she said that her family wouldn't help except for her sister, whose husband would not help."

Jack didn't say anything, but the air around him changed, and she knew he was furious. Violet nudged the coffee in his hand. Too little sleep and not enough coffee combined with anger wasn't a good combination for the most tolerant and understanding of men. Violet loved every inch of her oversized husband, and he was not tolerant of men without honor.

When Jack's face didn't ease, Violet crawled onto his lap, taking his face between her hands. "Breathe, darling."

It took him a long moment to respond and she felt his jaw flex under her hands. She ran her thumb back and forth, striving to soothe him but uncertain if she'd achieved it. She hummed low and then lifted one finger to press against the wrinkle between his brows.

His eyes glinted with humor and he said, "I'm not

going to storm across the hall and teach Liam Hanson the lesson he deserves."

"That's good darling, as you'd alarm Margaret Hanson. Mr. Baldwin forced the rogue away, and she's alone."

"Where did he go?" Jack's voice was dangerous and Vi hesitated to answer. There was a rescuing knight in him, but sometimes he forgot that he could only protect while he was present. The long term protection was only possible with Margaret's help.

"I don't know," Vi admitted. "Perhaps the gentlemen's smoking room?"

Jack considered. "He seemed in his cups. When you're witless from drink, anywhere is possible. It wouldn't even be surprising to find him sleeping across the counter in the bath, or in one of those lounge chairs."

Violet shrugged, hoping that wherever the man had slept, it had been uncomfortable and cold. She hoped he would wake as stiff as his wife and possibly Mr. Baldwin. She hoped he got a seasonal cold from the chill and it lingered for weeks, reminding him of the type of man he'd been and what he'd done to the woman who should have been able to trust him.

"Vi darling," Jack said and then paused. He continued, "Check on her, would you? See if she needs a safe place to sleep while she recovers? We could give her our cabin for the day. Aspirin, perhaps?"

Vi pushed up on her knees and kissed his cheek. It was the man who thought of the little things that she'd fallen in love with. It was his penetrating gaze that knew her and *loved* her. What was more intoxicating than a man who wanted her for *her*? Absolutely nothing.

Violet dressed easily. One of her favorite nude rose dresses that set off her complexion, a quick brush through her hair and then a turban over it. Stockings, comfortable shoes, and a lacy cardigan to keep her warm. Vi left off all jewels but placed a silk scarf around her neck. With the breeze off the ocean, she wanted something more. She put on the barest trace of pink lipstick, decided she looked presentable enough to be seen by anyone other than her family and crossed to the cabin across the way.

Vi knocked and there was no answer. Her mouth twisted and she glanced at Pederson whose head slipped out of the little compartment for stewards as they looked at the door together.

"Did she answer for you before?"

Pederson shook his head.

"Did you take the coffee away or did she take it in?"

"She took it in," he replied. "I added aspirin and then I was called to assist an elderly passenger. When I came back, it was gone."

"The aspirin was clever," Violet said, deciding that Pederson and Baldwin would both be getting a large something rather than a little something. "You're a good man, Pederson."

He blushed lightly and nodded and then Vi knocked again.

"Mrs. Hanson?" Vi called. "Mrs. Hanson? It's Mrs. Wakefield."

There was nothing. For no reason, whatsoever, Vi felt a chill. "No one has seen her yet?"

"I saw several stop by this morning," Pederson said low, whispering the confidence that he shouldn't share, but they were both worried. "The twin sister, her husband, some blonde with curly hair, a dark-haired fellow. It's been a regular train."

"Perhaps she thinks it is us." Vi paused and then asked suddenly, "Was her twin with her husband when they visited or did Mrs. Nielsen come alone?"

"She came alone." Pederson frowned. "Does that matter?"

Vi started to shake her head, but she couldn't. If Violet were hurting and Victor had come by, Violet would have swung the door open and told him everything. She knew they were close, closer than most siblings, but Vi thought back to the way that Ruth Nielsen had easily cut off her brother-in-law and protected her twin. Ruth knew what Margaret was experiencing.

"Did she know what had happened?" Vi asked. What did that matter? Vi bit down on her lip and fiddled with her wedding ring.

"I don't know, ma'am." He considered, his dark eyes meeting Vi's. He was a hulking Norwegian with inexplicably dark eyes.

"I think we had better open this door," Violet told him flatly. "Just to be sure."

"I—"

"I will take full responsibility," Violet told him. "Should it come down to it, you can step away to help someone else, and I'll just take your keys."

His gaze widened and then he blushed as he handed her his keys. "What shall I say I was doing?"

"Go get my husband fresh coffee," Violet told him. "Perhaps aspirin and toast for a hangover."

He nodded and disappeared and Violet waited until she counted to thirty and then slipped the key into the lock, knocking as she did so. There was no answer. Violet bit down on her bottom lip even as she straightened her shoulders and then she opened the door.

"Mrs. Hanson?"

There was no answer.

"Mrs. Hanson?"

Again, no answer. Violet considered leaving and then stepped inside. When would she get a chance to snoop again? She had no respect for privacy, Violet scolded herself. But when she took another step into the room, she saw a pair of shoes lying on the floor near the bed. They were lying on their side, which paused Violet as her mind caught up with what she was seeing.

The shoes were in feet. And the feet were attached to legs. And the legs were attached to a lovely torso. The robe Mrs. Hanson was wearing covered only a silk nightgown. It was cut low, and Violet could see a dark bruise on the chest between Mrs. Hanson's breasts with the bruise edging more towards the left.

Vi winced and then saw another dark bruise on Mrs. Hanson's thigh. Vi had stopped breathing and she dropped to her knees next to the woman, pushing her onto her back, eyes welling with tears when Vi saw the woman's chest move.

A low groan filled the air and Vi squeaked. Her squeak was followed by a scream, "Jack!"

She knew he would come and so she checked Mrs. Hanson for some wound, some terrible injury that Vi could attend to, but there was nothing. Vi frowned as the door to the compartment banged open and Jack dropped down next to her.

"Where is he?" Jack growled.

"He's not here," Violet whispered. "Jack! She's alive!"

He started and then lifted her into his arms. "The doctor!"

Vi considered the words of Baldwin the night before, but she didn't let them delay her. She hurried to the steward's compartment. There was a telephone and Vi connected herself to the doctor's compartment. There was no answer.

She tried again.

Nothing.

She tried again.

Again, there was nothing, so she looked at the other connections and tried the captain's cabin instead. Finally an answer. Vi explained, begging for help and then abandoning the line for her husband and the poor Margaret Hanson.

Had Violet done this? Had Violet somehow pointed out the lack of options for Mrs. Hanson and made her want to end things? Or…perhaps someone else had tried to end things instead. What if there wasn't a wound not because there had been no ill-intent but because the instrument of death hadn't been a knife or a gun but a poison?

A flock of stewards arrived with an elderly and drunken doctor and Vi's gaze narrowed on the man.

"Oh ho," he said almost cheerily. "Sea-sickness?"

Jack turned towards Violet, eyed her and then said, "Not sea-sickness."

"Oh?" The doctor blinked blearily at Jack. Then his

watery, ancient eyes glanced down at the body of Margaret Hanson breathing shallowly on the bed. He frowned. "She doesn't seem well."

"We think she may have been poisoned," Violet told him flatly.

Those old eyes widened and then filled with doubt.

Jack, however, repeated firmly, "Poison."

Neither of them said whether they thought it was self-administered or nefariously-administered.

"Poison," the doctor repeated.

He leaned down and Vi saw his hands were shaking. Did he have some sort of palsy or was he simply needing a drink? Vi saw Pederson in the hall and then crossed to him asking quietly, "Is he a drunkard?"

Pederson's gaze widened and then he nodded once. Vi reached out, and squeezed Pederson's forearm and then returned to Jack. She pushed up on her toes and whispered into his ear and her already stiff Jack turned to stone.

Jack waved the stewards out of the room, somehow taking command, and sent one of them for Hamilton Barnes. He sent another for the captain of the ship. And he sent a third for Kate Carlyle and her nanny. It was Jack who lifted Mrs. Hanson in his arms and started towards the area of the ship used as a sick bay. He looked back at Vi, and she mouthed, "the twin."

She didn't follow and Jack nodded once. He understood. He wasn't happy to be separated until they were certain she was safe, but she knew better than to accept a drink from some random fellow, and whoever poisoned Mrs. Hanson—if it wasn't herself—had no reason to hurt Vi.

CHAPTER 8

*V*iolet hurried through the ship towards the area where the keys were mounted to a large board with hooks. There was generally a steward nearby, and she intended to demand from him which cabin belonged to the Nielsens. Before she reached the board, however, Rita came darting up.

"Jack sent me."

"So protective," Vi muttered. She hooked her arm through Rita's. "Do you know where the Nielsen twin is?"

Rita nodded. As they hurried through the ship, Violet explained what had happened since she'd last seen Rita.

"Do you think she tried to kill herself?"

It wouldn't be the first time a woman had decided to die rather than continue with one such as Liam Hanson. Violet remembered Margaret's words. *I'm far past a little thought and everything I have to give.* Margaret had been hopeless the night before. It was possible she'd found something to make it all stop. Bruised and tired, it might have been the best choice as far as she was able to see.

Vi knew about grey days and blue outlooks. She knew about that feel in the air as though all that was there was darkness. The way it seemed so difficult to just move your arms. The way that things that usually made her happy brought smiles only by reflex. She had pretended to be happy more than once.

Had Margaret done the same but had enough of the struggle? Vi shivered. She never, ever wanted to do to *her* twin what Violet was about to do to Ruth. Rita stopped outside the door of the cabin, and the two friends met each other's gazes. They were about to ruin Ruth's day.

Vi considered how she'd feel if she lost Victor. It would never be the same again. Things would never be as bright. As deeply, as horrifically as Violet missed her great-aunt, it was possible to find good things. She'd expected to eventually lose Aunt Agatha. But Victor, Vi shook her head, rejecting the thought immediately.

Of course, Margaret wasn't dead. Vi prayed and then knocked on the door. There was no answer. This time, however, Vi sighed with relief. She knocked again.

"Mrs. Nielsen?"

Rita walked towards the steward's compartment as Violet knocked again.

"Mrs. Nielsen?" Vi called. The relief was growing. Mrs. Nielsen was elsewhere. She didn't know her sister was struggling to survive. She didn't know. Now, perhaps, it would be someone else's turn to tell the woman of her sister's condition. Someone who *wasn't* Vi. Someone who *wasn't* a twin. Someone who wouldn't project the trouble of the one twin on the other.

Violet knocked again. "Mrs. Nielsen?"

There was no answer, but she heard Rita say, "The steward says she's in there."

Vi closed her eyes, her hopes fading.

"I told him what happened," Rita said carefully, understanding her friend too well. "He's going to open up the cabin in case she's sleeping deeply."

The steward stepped forward and Vi stepped back, whispering to Rita, "I had hoped…"

She didn't complete the thought, but Rita took hold of Vi's hand and squeezed. The steward knocked again before he turned the handle and then opened the door. Mrs. Nielsen was on the bed, another open robe, but she at least, was wearing full pajamas.

"Would you wake her, ma'am?" The steward stepped back, and Vi didn't blame him. She would rather be woken by someone she knew peripherally than a strange man.

Violet sighed and then took in a deep breath. She reached out a hand, trembling in advance for Mrs. Nielsen and then shook her shoulder.

There was no reply.

Vi frowned and glanced at Rita who reached out and tried for the second time. When Mrs. Nielsen didn't wake, Vi gasped and then reached out and tried a third time, shaking the woman fiercely. A nearly identical moan to earlier occurred and Vi closed her eyes.

"I think whatever is wrong with Mrs. Hanson may be wrong with Mrs. Nielsen."

The statement echoed in the chamber and was almost impossible to believe. Two women poisoned? What were the chances? Vi found herself skipping through motives.

Had the women inherited money and they were suddenly worth more dead than alive? Had the sisters seen something and a criminal needed them silenced? Had the partners decided to rid themselves of their wives and then fight over the curvy blonde?

"We need the doctor," the steward said with a wince that declared he, too, knew the doctor was a drunkard.

"He's busy," Vi said almost absently. "We'll need to take her to him."

The steward wasn't particularly large, but he seemed up to the task. He lifted Mrs. Nielsen and Violet and Rita went before and behind to clear the way and keep those who would interfere back. Down the lift, down a passageway, and through a rather terrible looking door that once was white but had become dingy with age.

Inside, Jack looked up first. He took in the sight in a moment and then glanced at Ham who was watching the doctor. Jack cleared his throat, somehow telling Ham that something was wrong without needing to explain.

Ham looked up, saw his wife, saw the steward, and then saw Mrs. Nielsen. "Bloody hell."

Jack seemed to agree though he said nothing.

"Bloody, bloody hell," Ham said again. His gaze met the captain's and then crossed to him. There was a deep dark sigh and then Ham pulled the captain from the room.

The doctor turned when Kate's nanny, Jane, ordered, "Examine the new patient, doctor."

Vi's brows lifted and Kate said, "She was a nurse before she turned to nannying. She said after the Great War she wanted to spend more time with life than death."

Vi felt a rush of relief. Nanny Jane wasn't a woman

who would let the doctor make mistakes if she could stop him.

"What is to be done?" Vi asked the nanny, ignoring the doctor.

She paused. "I think it might be a dose of arsenic."

"But she's not dead," Rita said. "I thought that would kill you."

"It must have been too small a dose to be successful," she said. "You can survive such a thing if you don't take enough."

"But what are the chances that this was self-administered considering it's both of them?"

Nanny shrugged. "That isn't a question for me, ma'am."

Violet looked to Kate. "Have you been conscripted to looking after the patient…" Vi winced. "…patients."

"I'm here to lend weight," Kate told Vi. "Nanny is the real nurse. I'm here to channel your stepmother and imperiously order things around. I don't believe, however, that Jack intends for us to be alone without himself, Victor, or Ham."

"Where is Victor?" Vi asked, wanting desperately to see her twin and know he was well.

"He and Denny have the babies," Kate replied. "Nanny Jane was having her breakfast while Nanny Poppy stayed with the babies. Now Nanny Poppy will be in charge of the three of them while Nanny Jane sees to the patients."

Nanny Jane was putting an IV in each of the women's arms. The doctor started to object, but Nanny Jane snorted. "Look at those hands of yours, doctor. You should be ashamed of yourself."

The doctor blushed darkly and started to snap a reply,

but Jack placed a hand on the man's shoulder. Jack didn't squeeze but they could all see his hands shaking, and the doctor couldn't argue otherwise.

"Good of you to be here, nurse," the doctor said, striving for his place of power, but he was ignored. His blush turned to fury, but this time Jack did squeeze. Not hard, Vi was sure, but with enough firmness to ensure the doctor knew where the real power lay, and it wasn't with Nanny Jane or the drunk doctor.

"And where are the husbands?" Rita asked low, looking at the two women.

"The captain sent several of the stewards looking for them."

Vi didn't care about them. Except, she thought, the chances of this being some sort of suicide pact.

"Ma'am," Nanny Jane said. "Sir."

Nanny Jane glanced around the room, drawing attention to everyone but the doctor.

"Look at Mrs. Hanson," the nanny said. "Her heart is racing. She has messed herself."

The nanny must have cleaned Mrs. Hanson while Violet was out of the room.

"Her stomach is clenching. She didn't make it to her bed. Was that because she passed out or because she lost her balance? I wouldn't be surprised if this is arsenic poisoning. Given that she's not dead, she might well survive. Time will tell."

Vi winced. Arsenic. It was the easy answer for someone who would poison. Something everyone who had read a Christie novel would think of.

"Was Mrs. Nielsen poisoned with arsenic as well?" Vi

asked absently. What else could it be? To her surprise, however, Nanny Jane cleared her throat.

"I don't think so."

"Really?" Kate gasped. "Whatever else could it be?"

"Look at her," Nanny started and the doctor scoffed.

"What do you know of it? A nurse who hasn't practiced for years?"

"I read medical books," Nanny Jane said to Kate. Vi's sister-in-law reached out and squeezed the nanny's hand.

"I am well aware of how much knowledge one might acquire with an eager mind and good books," Kate told Nanny simply.

The doctor scoffed but Jack said, "Enough."

The threat wasn't in the words, but the tone, and Vi ignored both her beloved and the idiot doctor.

"Please explain, Nanny," Kate said.

Nanny nodded. She was entirely unruffled by the doctor. She simply gestured, "Mrs. Nielsen is having convulsions. They're slight compared to what she might have had earlier before you found her. She's got dilated pupils, and it seems some muscle paralysis. I'm not entirely certain she's unaware. She might just be locked in her body."

Vi gasped in horror and only recognized a moment later that she was one of a chorus between herself, Kate, and Rita.

"What do you think it is?" Jack asked Nanny Jane.

"I believe it is hemlock."

They all stared at her.

"For Mrs. Nielsen, she might be in danger yet. Only time will tell. For Mrs. Hanson, I believe she'll survive."

Violet glanced around, sickly. "Where are the husbands?"

There was no reply since they had no idea. Jack met Vi's gaze and then Vi said, "What about the curvy blonde woman? Has anyone checked her cabin?"

"Mrs. Kristiansen?" Rita asked. Conviction filled her gaze and Vi agreed. They both glanced at Jack who said, "Neither of you are going. I'm sure Ham has come to the same conclusion."

Vi glanced at Rita and the two of them knew that the gents had already discussed the same idea. While Rita and Vi had been looking for the twin sister, before they realized she was also a victim, Ham and Jack had thought ahead.

"Detectives," Rita muttered darkly.

"You can take the man out of Scotland Yard," Vi added, trailing off. She didn't need to complete the thought, but Jack rolled his eyes at her as if she had.

CHAPTER 9

Vi and Rita left the sick bay with Jack. He had leaned down before they left and whispered into the doctor's ear. The man had scowled and squeaked and objected, but before they left, he had made his way into the corner of the sick bay and sat with his arms crossed over his chest like a child in a dunce's cap.

They found Denny in the passageway with a steward who had refused to let him pass.

"I wasn't invited to the party," Denny scowled. "But I found the abusive husband."

Jack's brows rose.

"I had an idea and I left the babies with Victor and Lila. She told me it wasn't a burden to her to rock a baby, but if I thought she was going to do more than look on in interest while we meddled, I was very wrong."

"Why would she even say that?" Rita asked, unable to keep from laughing. "She rarely does anything but sit back languidly and look pretty."

"She scolds!" Denny's defensive tone prompted another round of inappropriate laughter.

"Oh Denny," Vi told him. "You do brighten my day."

"Rather like a puppy," Rita told him before he was too happy by the compliment. They grinned at each other like squabbling siblings.

Rita wore a light blue dress with scalloped edges that hung loosely on her form, attempting and failing to give her the lines of a mannish figure. Rita was far too voluptuous for such disguises, but she did look expensive and beautiful.

"You know," Vi told Rita, "you're pretty and expensive like Victor."

Denny giggled. "Ah, our other courtesan."

They reached the portion of the ship with the gymnasium and then found the empty steam room. Inside of it lay Liam Hanson. Vi considered waking him with a swift kick, but he was balanced so precariously on the too small bench that she decided instead to reach out a solitary finger, place it against his shoulder, and push.

He rolled and splatted hard against the floor. Vi jumped back as he was falling and grinned at Jack at the sight of the moaning Mr. Hanson.

Jack's gaze was filled with humor, but his voice was mean when he said, "Wake up, Hanson!"

Mr. Hanson's reply was more croak than speech.

"Hanson!" Jack nudged the man with the toe of his shoe, and he wasn't gentle about it. "Wake up!"

Slowly, Mr. Hanson opened bloodshot eyes. Jack told him, "Get up."

"Here now," Hanson groaned. "What's the big idea?"

"Get up," Jack said with an ice cold fury that had

Hanson scowling, but standing. As he measured himself against Jack and realized just how lacking he was, Hanson adjusted his stance from aggressive to defensive.

"What's going on?" Mr. Hanson asked.

"Your wife is potentially dying. Not that we expected you to be sympathetic."

"Maggie?" Hanson demanded, actually sounding upset. "My Maggie?"

"Your punching bag?" Denny countered. "Yes. She's in the sick bay, and you're the main suspect."

"Me?" Hanson asked. He seemed genuinely confused, and Violet had to wonder if he was entirely unaware of how others viewed him.

"You," Denny snapped. "Even I think that. You're a right prick of a husband and a shame to mankind."

If Jack hadn't been there, Hanson would have attacked Denny. He almost lunged and he had to wipe his hand over his mouth before he collected himself. He left a smear of something behind and then wiped again, using his sleeve as his handkerchief.

"By Jove," Jack told him. "We've seen the bruises on your wife."

Hanson's ears turned red with fury, and he ground out, "How did you *see* any such thing?"

"So you don't deny them?" Rita asked silkily. "The deep aching marks you left on *your Maggie?*"

"His punching bag," Denny countered. "Don't act like he loves her."

"I do love her," Hanson said defensively.

"Do you?" Jack asked. "Love her and bruise her?"

"How did you see her…" Hanson was furious that the

bruises had been seen, but he didn't want to admit they were there.

"The marks of your affection," Denny goaded. He grinned at Hanson when the man turned an angry gaze on Denny. Comfortable in the security of Jack, Denny added again, "I saw that deep one on her breast."

That was too much for Hanson and he lunged at Denny, hands out in a grasping manner that said he'd have wrung the life out of Denny's neck if given the chance. Denny stepped back as Jack held out a strong arm and clotheslined the abusive Hanson. The man hit the wall of Jack's arm, flew back, and ended on his back, winded.

Jack put his hand on the man's wrist and pressed on it meanly. There was no gentleness, no kindness, no mercy in her husband. Vi wondered if she should be afraid, but she knew that she never would be. There would never be a time that Vi feared Jack. Drunk, furious, enraged, jealous, maddened, and he'd still be safe for Vi.

"You will be still," Jack told Hanson. "You will listen. Your wife has been poisoned. You are, of course, the main suspect. I am going to remove my foot from your wrist, you will stand up, and then you will walk like a man, or I will truss you like a baby and drag you behind me like you deserve."

Hanson gaped at Jack, feebly jerking at his wrist. "I...I..."

Jack waited, still, his gaze on Hanson. The two men stared each other down and then Hanson stuttered, "All right."

Jack slowly removed his foot and then they watched Hanson try to rise. He failed. He tried again and stumbled back. Slowly, Hanson turned onto his hands and knees and pulled himself up with the bench like a feeble old man who was too weak to stand up on his own.

He turned and faced them. "Maggie is dying?"

There was a bit of a plea in those words. A bit of a begging that none of them could answer.

"Perhaps," Violet told him without sympathy, "she might survive. Her prospects are…" Vi started to tell him of Mrs. Nielsen, but she didn't think he deserved the knowledge. "Hopeful is not the right word, but something approaching that."

"Thank God," Hanson said, and it seemed as though he felt it.

"She might have the strength to leave you now," Violet told him without mercy.

Hanson started and his gaze turned to Violet. There was a plea in it, but Violet wouldn't comfort him even if she could. She wouldn't. Never. Not for one such as him.

"She won't leave me," he said fiercely, and there was a threat in it. Jack didn't react, but Denny put out his foot and tripped the man. He went down hard, landing on his knees, and gasping in pain.

Denny's gaze wasn't amused, but he acknowledged what he'd done. "Sorry, old chap."

The tone was disgusted and Hanson heard the undisguised hatred in it. He pushed up, using the wall to help him, and then he said, "She'll live."

It was a prayer, and Vi marveled at it. They were moving towards the brig, which oddly was quite near the sick bay. Vi couldn't help but question the prayer. "You love her?"

"Of course I do," Hanson said, looking at Vi as though she were an idiot. "She's my wife, isn't she?"

"Who is covered in bruises from your hands," Violet countered. She kept her tone even and fairly gentle. He didn't deserve it from her, the gentleness. But she wanted answers. "I don't understand how you can say you love her."

"I don't need your approval, idiot woman," Hanson snapped at her, viciously. Like Denny, she was unafraid of the man with Jack there. Jack reached out a hand, settling it as a heavy weight on Hanson's shoulders and he muttered low to himself, a continual woebegone diatribe that demanded understanding. He would never get it from those present.

When Jack reached the brig, he glanced in and turned and explained. "Ham beat us with Nielsen. The captain and first officer are present. They're not going to let you join in."

It was directed at Vi, but Denny and Rita were included as well. As Jack and Hanson left, Vi found herself surprised to be cursing and then she said, "I want to see Victor."

Rita wrapped her hand around Vi's waist and said, "*Your* twin is fine."

Vi nodded, knowing it was true, but nothing would do for her but to see him herself, to know that he was all right, to see for herself. She moved without pausing, working her way towards her brother as Denny and Rita followed, whispering together. Vi reached the cabin that was in between Denny and Lila on the one side. On the other side was Victor and Kate. In between was the cabin that had been meant for two nannies, three babies. It was Vi's destination.

Vi knocked lightly, unconsciously using the patter that she and Victor had used as children. He knocked a reply, opened the door, and she threw herself at him, squeezing tightly.

He squeezed back and they whispered half-phrases, saying nothing, but conveying everything. After too long, Vivi started crying and Vi pulled back. She wasn't surprised to find her face wet with tears from the pain that hadn't happened but that she could imagine only too well after today.

"You can't die first," she told Victor.

"All right," he said agreeably and then glanced at Denny. "There's ginger wine in my cabin." Vi curled up on one of the neatly made beds, lifting baby Vivi, and holding her as tightly as the baby would allow. A squawk disciplined Vi, and she pulled back. Vivi and Agatha were old enough to babble and Vi listened to the scolding she deserved and answered seriously.

"Are they going to live?" Victor asked.

Vi hesitated long enough to make it clear no one knew. Their gazes met again, and they conversed almost silently. Each of them held one of the twins and then Vi said, "I need to walk. Perhaps the girls need to get some air?"

Victor left with Vi and she told him all she knew. They fell silent when she reached the end of the tale and then Vi confessed, "I'm starving."

Victor snorted and led the way to the dining room. Vi ordered a full English breakfast with scones and Turkish coffee and Victor echoed the order even though he'd eaten long before. Vi started with the tomatoes, sharing with Vivi who demanded bites between Vi's. She finally handed Vivi the toast and let her make a mangle of it while she ate what she could before Vivi stole more.

When Vi had finished she said, "Don't die, all right?"

"All right," Victor agreed. Baby Agatha had his piece of toast in her hand. Somehow, Agatha was a lady taking nibbles off the toast while Vivi smeared her face, dress, and Violet with butter and crumbs. "You're going to get in trouble for that dress from Nanny Poppy."

"I'll buy her another," Vi swore. She looked at her own dress and admitted, "And probably one for me as well."

"Are you all right, Vi?"

Vi thought back to the hopeless gaze she'd seen from Margaret the night before. Then to the moment of certainty when she'd seen Margaret's body and thought that her husband had returned to finish the job, and then the horror when she realized Margaret was yet alive. Vi had been terrified she'd have to watch another person die. She had seen breath stop before. She had seen the transition from alive to dead. The way something essential left the body and with that, whatever had made the person who they were was gone.

Violet bit down on her bottom lip and asked, "Why would someone try to murder the two of them?"

Victor's head tilted. "If this were a book, I would say that they have money. Maybe money that more than one person would inherit. Something that we could stack up as a reason. A motive. Filthy lucre and all that."

Vi stared at him, and he stared back. Their aunt had died in just such a manner. It was interesting when it was a mystery novel and quite terrible when it was your life and the people you loved.

"I wonder if they were in England for something," Vi said. "A funeral of a rich aunt."

"There's always a rich aunt," Victor said sardonically. "Some well-off old maid or widow without children of her own."

"Always," Vi agreed without humor. She thought back to the tender gaze of her great-aunt. The woman who had loved them from babyhood to adulthood. The woman who had provided the example of what to be. The woman that Vi considered when she was lost in her thoughts. *What would Aunt Agatha do* was the question that ruled Vi's mind. She was their mother in all the ways that mattered except by birth. She had raised the twins, and when she had died...no, when she had been murdered, she had changed their lives by bequeathing on them their fortunes.

Their gazes met again with shared, soul-deep pain. Slowly Vi breathed in, shuddering for the both of them as Victor buried his own feelings.

"She'd have loved to have your baby named after her," Violet told him. "She'd have adored Kate and reminded you endlessly that you married above your station."

"I did," Victor said easily. "Any idiot could see that, even this idiot."

They grinned at each other and Violet said, "But you know what doesn't make sense?"

Victor nodded. "The two poisons. If you want to rid yourself of the twins, why not poison them both, at the same time?"

"Why not?" Vi agreed.

"It doesn't make sense to do them separately," Victor added. "That's twice the opportunity to be caught. Twice the opportunity for witnesses."

Vi nodded, tapping her chin. Baby Vivi shrieked an unholy, eardrum breaking howl that had people turning in their tables to shoot dark glances at Vi and Victor.

"That's our cue to leave," Victor said. He rose, took Vivi, and gave Vi the chance to brush the mess Vivi had made off of herself.

They headed away from their table and then Vi paused in the doorway and said, "It doesn't make sense," Vi agreed. "Unless of course we have two poisoners."

Victor scoffed, but the idea settled on them both and they were silent as they made their way back to the temporary nursery and left the twins with the nanny. Their gazes met. Jack was helping Ham and the captain. Kate was monitoring the poison victims.

"Your cabin or mine?" Victor asked lightly.

"Do you have more wine?"

"I do indeed. And our manuscript."

No further answer was needed.

CHAPTER 10

*V*i met Rita in the dining room for a late luncheon. Afterwards, they visited the sick bay. Though they were interested in how the twins were doing, each of them wanted to know if their husbands were yet working.

There was a steward in front of the brig door, and Violet and Rita weren't allowed to do anything other than ask after their husbands. They were only told that their husbands were still busy and would be told that they had visited.

The sick bay contained Nanny Jane, the doctor, Kate reading a book to Mrs. Nielsen, and Victor, who watched his wife with affection and love.

"How are they?" Vi asked, crossing to Kate.

She looked up from reading *Dr. Thorne* to the poor women and paused. "Mrs. Nielsen may be doing better. Mrs. Hanson has woken, but she doesn't stay awake, and she can't speak. She saw her sister, panicked, and fainted."

"Nanny, will they live?"

Nanny Jane paused and then said, "I think so."

"How did they both survive?" Vi asked.

"Perhaps it was strong blood," Nanny mused, ignoring the snort of the doctor. "Or perhaps they had a very poor poisoner."

Vi snorted and leaned back. She reached out and took hold of Mrs. Hanson's wrist. "These poor women. Something occurred to Vi and she added, "These poor twins. Surely, we can move them closer together?"

Violet looked at the two hospital beds and then she took off the brakes and moved them closer together, dropping the sides so they could sense the other's presence. Violet stared down at the two sisters and wished that more could be done for them.

"Is there nothing else that we can do?"

Nanny Jane said, "Not here. Not with him." Her gaze moved to the doctor.

He grunted, offended, but he cared far less about the jab now that it had been so long between drinks. Vi would have thought that he'd be demanding a drink or getting one for himself. Were they keeping the doctor from his self-medicine?

Violet didn't care, but she examined him. The man was sweating now and he looked as though he were about to sick up. His feet were moving restlessly and his hands were opening and closing as though he were going to strangle something.

Vi looked towards the nanny who eyed the doctor and then met Vi's gaze. Nanny nodded once for Vi's unasked question. Yes, the doctor was suffering. Yes, the nanny had an eye on him. Violet looked towards her brother who was lounging, but she saw that his gaze was fixed on the doctor's hands too.

"Why can't he have a drink?"

"Jack castigated the ship's captain for allowing a drunk doctor on ship. Told the captain that if either of the women died, it could be laid at his feet as well as the poisoner's." Kate had paused from reading to explain.

Vi wasn't surprised to hear it. Her husband was protective in the extreme, and his very soul would have been horrified to see that they'd been saddled with a man who couldn't make it a few hours without a drink. Surely the captain had known? If he hadn't, he was just as responsible for what happened because it was his duty to know and to protect his passengers.

Vi took a seat next to Victor because she didn't have anything else to do. She fell into the story as the moments passed and finally there was a knock at the door of the sick bay. Rita rose to answer the door and then she stepped back.

Her eyes were alight with interest as she let Mrs. Kristiansen into the room. Vi lifted a brow and glanced at her twin. They were, the both of them, disgusted to see the lover of the man who wouldn't attend the possible deathbed of his wife.

"Why are you here?" Vi had little patience for pretending. Not in the face of the two women. Not while her lover's wife lay there, unable to speak, but possibly aware. Vi would speak for the wife, for Mrs. Ruth Nielsen who had married and left her country, who had brought her twin along, who had watched her twin abused and was refused help from the man who was supposed to love her. How could he love her while he also loved Mrs. Kristiansen?

"I am here to see my friends. Why are *you* here?" It was a challenge and a declaration. Of them all, Mrs. Kristiansen had the most right to be there, and she intended to exercise it.

Vi lifted her brow again, letting the little blonde meet her gaze. Vi had only seen the woman from a distance before now. In person, Mrs. Kristiansen was sensuousness personified. She wasn't lovelier than either of the twins, but she seemed to exude a lascivious interest in the world around. No, Vi thought, the men around. Mrs. Kristiansen rejected the doctor in a moment and then her gaze moved to Victor.

"I don't think so," Kate said mildly, closing her book.

Victor cleared his throat and shot his wife a look that said he could be trusted even when she wasn't present. Kate didn't doubt Victor, but she wasn't going to watch the woman throw herself at her husband while she stood there.

"Pardon?" Mrs. Kristiansen asked innocently. She even fluttered her lashes. For all their foolish expressions, Vi's friends only used a lash flutter ironically. The poor woman didn't understand the round of humor that was barely held back, but she could tell they were laughing at her, and she flushed prettily. Her gaze returned again to Victor and he crossed his arms over his chest defensively.

Vi wondered if it was an act, this innocence, or if Mrs. Kristiansen was just naturally focused on men. Did she just not see the women around her? Did Mrs. Kristiansen turn her wiles towards the men and not even realize what she was doing? Vi examined the lover and then thought, no. This woman wasn't quite so innocent as that.

Violet's head cocked. "You'll find my brother isn't as easy a mark as Mr. Nielsen."

Mrs. Kristiansen blinked innocently. "I'm sure I don't know what you mean."

"Darling," Rita inserted, "surely you realize that none of us are going to allow you such an act. You are the lover of the husband of the woman there. We all know it, and none of us will let you pretend. Not in front of her deathbed."

Mrs. Kristiansen gasped and her eyes teared prettily. It was the type of move that for other people would have a man tucking her close and comforting her.

"I wonder," Violet asked, "if Mrs. Nielsen believes you. She's aware, did you know? Lying there locked in her body and able to hear your lies. I wonder what she would say if she were able to speak."

Vi hadn't been sure, but Mrs. Nielsen's eyes fluttered and a look of horror crossed Mrs. Kristiansen's face. The movement of the eyes was enough to make Vi's statement believable even to herself.

Mrs. Kristiansen shook her head. "She can't be. Surely she is sleeping?"

"I don't believe so," Nanny Jane said firmly. "She's awake at the moment. Awake and in pain."

"She's going to live," Vi said. She hoped she didn't lie, but she was afraid she did. "*Your* poisoning of your lover's wife was unsuccessful."

Mrs. Kristiansen's jaw dropped and a look of shock

crossed her face. She seemed almost confused. "Poisoning? I thought they fell ill?"

"Ill of poison," Rita said.

Vi considered and then added, "Or perhaps your lover is getting rid of his wife, and you are innocent? Perhaps, in fact, it will be your fate in the future."

"That's not possible," Mrs. Kristiansen hissed. Even if her lover had poisoned his wife, she didn't believe he would ever hurt her. Vi was sure that Mrs. Nielsen had once wanted to believe the same.

"Why?" Rita demanded. "Because your lover was with you while his wife lay poisoned and alone?"

Mrs. Kristiansen shook her head mutely, but it wasn't a denial of Rita's suggestion but a horror-filled plea.

"You know, of course, he's being questioned right now."

"That doesn't mean anything. Maybe their friend poisoned them," Mrs. Kristiansen shot out, desperately. "Why would Oskar try to kill Margaret as well? They need her."

Vi perked with interest. "Do they?"

A look of defiance crossed Mrs. Kristiansen's face and she said, "He *was* with me. It must have been someone else."

"Not," Rita countered, "if the poison was put in something that would get them eventually. The poisoning is done while they're elsewhere, and then the man seeks an alibi for when it strikes."

"He wouldn't," Mrs. Kristiansen said even more firmly.

She had doubted for a moment, Vi thought, but that doubt had faded. "Wouldn't he? Why are you so sure?"

"The shipping company is a partnership," Mrs. Kristiansen said with scorn, tossing her pretty curls and letting her gaze stray to Victor again. "Oskar, Liam, my father, and their father. If both of the twins are dead, Mr. North will remove himself from the company. He's an old-fashioned man. He doesn't like that they married Norwegians, but he believes in supporting his children. That will change if they're gone. Oskar would *never* risk his company. He would never poison the twins."

Vi noted the plural and wondered what Mrs. Kristiansen would say if just one of them lay struggling for her life rather than both. What then? Would she accept and wonder? Would she continue in his bed with the theory that he had killed a previous occupant or would she be wise enough to escape before it was too late.

Violet lifted a brow and asked a different question, "And their father doesn't care that Liam is abusive?"

Mrs. Kristiansen glanced aside and then muttered, "I don't believe he knows."

Vi's head tilted at that. If that fiend Liam had kept his actions hidden while they were in England, then perhaps the daughters were guessing wrong about their father. Her gaze strayed to her friend and landed on Victor who was wondering the same thing. She knew him too well, and he was calculating the same thing she was.

"I find myself wondering if these twins are doubting their father when they shouldn't," Victor said. A natural conclusion for Violet and Victor, and their matching eyes met and remembered the same things. It had been a problem for them as well. Doubting their father, his love, what he would do for them. He had failed them as they'd been raised never knowing he cared, but he *did* care.

"I wonder if we would wire their father," Violet suggested. "I wonder how he would feel about husbands who lust after the same woman. I wonder how he'd feel about a son-in-law who hurts his daughter. How he'd feel about the way they use these girls for his money."

"We are storytellers," Victor suggested to Mrs. Kristiansen's mounting horror. She had more of a reaction to this idea than she did to the sight of the two women lying side-by-side. "We might be able to explain it correctly."

"A job for you," Kate said to her husband. "It will mean more coming from a man. An earl's son. Make sure you sign it as an honorable. Make sure you sound horrified and make it impinge on his honor. Suggest the righteous fury of a father to strike."

Victor snorted, but Vi knew he would do just that, simply because Kate had asked him to. These sisters wouldn't be worse off, physically at least, if their father knew the truth. It might destroy their faith in him if he didn't act, but it was worth the risk, Violet thought. After all, what if it did work? They needed an escape. Love from a father. A safe place. Perhaps it was a fairytale, but Vi wanted to believe.

And of course, if the sisters died, their father needed to know why they had died and where to strike. Also, Vi thought meanly, if they died, she wanted their father to know he'd contributed by not allowing them to be safe.

"Who is the friend?" Vi asked, changing the subject again. "The dark haired man?"

"Wenzel Wagner? The would-be poet?" Mrs. Kristiansen laughed and then muttered. "The Romeo who thought that dying for love was better than living?" Her expression was mean. "Idiot women."

Violet leaned back. They had a name for the fellow and a picture of Mrs. Kristiansen. Vi wanted to talk to the fellow, but she also wanted Mrs. Kristiansen to fear for comments such as that. She seemed to see the women as mere roadblocks to her own wants. "You know of course that if you didn't poison the wife, her husband did."

Mrs. Kristiansen shook her head. "Oskar isn't like that."

"What about Liam? He has an eye on you as well."

"Liam?" Mrs. Kristiansen's confident scoff was back. "I might pursue a married man. I might be amoral, but I am not completely dim. A man like Liam will hurt whoever he loves, and I'm not a person who wants pain in my life."

"He wants you," Rita said. "We can all see it."

"We don't always get what we want." Mrs. Kristiansen licked her dry lips and her gaze focused on the suffering twin sisters again. Sympathy passed over her face and she said, "Oskar didn't do this. Perhaps Liam did."

Violet thought that Mrs. Kristiansen believed her claim. She seemed firm, but Violet knew that people lied. Often to themselves. Violet fiddled with her ring as she considered. If Mrs. Kristiansen was lying to herself, it was because she didn't want to believe she had been wrong. She didn't want to admit she'd thrown herself at a married man, and he was a killer.

"What are your plans then? Just to carry on with the wife in the way?" Kate's voice was gentle as though she sympathized. Maybe Kate did.

"Oskar wants to divorce Ruth. They're not in love anymore, if they ever were."

Violet rolled her eyes, unimpressed. It was difficult to stay in love with a man who was straying and refused you the things you needed. A safe sister, a true husband, was it so hard to provide so little?

"He probably never loved her," Rita said, thinking more like Vi. "Ruth brought him money. He married her for his business. He's never going to marry you."

"He loves me."

"Is that enough?" Kate asked in the same gentle manner that had Mrs. Kristiansen tearing.

Rita wasn't any more gentle than Vi when she answered for Mrs. Kristiansen, "He loves money more than her, Kate. Their father doesn't sound like a man who keeps his money invested in a company of a man who abandons his daughter."

"He'd have stayed involved for Margaret," Mrs. Kristiansen shot out and then regretted it. Vi lifted both brows, gasping.

"I didn't mean that." Mrs. Kristiansen shuddered and then said, "I am not myself. I am in shock. My friends are dying, and I—"

"Well, you hope that one is dying," Rita answered, refusing the excuses. "You need the other."

The only answer was Mrs. Kristiansen letting out a cry, spinning on her feet, and rushing from the room.

*V*iolet crossed to the twins and leaned down to them. "I'm sorry."

Slowly Ruth Nielsen's eyes opened. Violet gasped and took her hand. She squeezed lightly in case she was in pain. Ruth was trying to speak and Violet asked her, "Can you blink?"

Slowly the woman blinked once.

"Can you blink twice?"

The woman blinked twice.

"Once for yes, twice for no."

She blinked once.

"Your sister has woken, but she's not really aware. It's only been half a day. There's hope since she's not dead yet."

Despair filled Ruth Nielsen's gaze and slowly tears leaked out of both eyes. Violet used her own handkerchief to mop them away.

"Do you want us to contact your father?"

It took Ruth Nielsen a long time to answer, but when she did, she blinked once.

"My brother will do it for you. Your father will respond to a man easier?"

Another solitary blink.

"It's good that you are awake and moving," Violet told her. "The nurse believes you've been poisoned with hemlock. You're getting better rather than worse. There's hope. Fight for yourself and your sister."

Ruth blinked once. If blinks could be fierce that one was and Violet was cheered, however mildly, to see it.

"We believe your sister was poisoned with arsenic."

The despair and the tears were back and Violet allowed Mrs. Nielsen her helpless cry. She tried and failed to speak and then Violet sighed.

"Should we talk to Wenzel?"

Ruth blinked and then she tried to speak again. Violet leaned closer to hear it and then leaned back frowning.

"Here?"

Ruth's frustrated gaze blinked once and then her gaze tried to turn to her sister.

"Here for your sister?"

Ruth blinked again.

Perhaps it was the case of the star-crossed lovers. Would Margaret recover better if she heard her lover reading to her rather than Kate? Violet nodded. "We'll find him."

"I'll find him now," Rita declared. "I won't fail you. Keep fighting, Ruth."

Ruth's gaze moved around the room and then she turned to Violet. They seemed to be asking a question, so

Violet sat with her and told the woman the story of the morning. When she was finished, Ruth closed her eyes and breathed deeply. She was trying to move and speak, Violet thought, but she was bound by the poison that had been administered.

When she'd heard that her husband was being questioned, she'd rolled her eyes. Didn't she fear him? Violet wondered about that and then about who Ruth thought had poisoned her and her sister. Violet asked, "Do you think it was Mrs. Kristiansen?"

Ruth didn't blink at all.

Vi sighed and then asked, "You don't know who did it?"

Ruth blinked once.

Violet leaned back fiddling with her wedding ring. She glanced at Victor who was writing something out on a paper and guessed it was the announcement of the daughters' predicament. She said, "It would have to be someone who knew you both."

"It would take knowledge of them to poison them like this," Kate said. "They were in different rooms, in different passageways. If it were some maniac, then it would be two different people poisoned."

"Agreed," Victor said. "That is what Ham said to the captain as well. It's why they've had those worthless husbands in the brig shooting questions at them for so long."

Violet listed the names out loud. "Oskar Nielsen. Liam Hanson. Wenzel Wagner. Milly Kristiansen." Vi turned to Ruth and asked, "Do you know anyone else aboard?"

Two blinks.

Violet nibbled on her lip and then rose to pace. She moved back and forth ignoring the doctor, the nanny, even the twins laying in suffering. Kate had gone back to reading to the women and Victor had gone back to scratching at his paper. Nanny Jane rose and checked the IV bags, took pulses and listened to hearts.

"Margaret Hanson seems a little better. Her heart rate has gone from thready to steady and not too fast."

"Wonderful," Violet said and then noticed that poor Ruth was crying again. Kate paused in her reading to mop the woman's tears. Violet returned to pacing.

The problem was the two poisons. *Why?* It wasn't like they were so easy to acquire. It wasn't like some English policeman wouldn't be able to try to find who had purchased them and why. He'd even be able to include descriptions of the four suspects. How much easier would it be to go into a chemist shop with a photograph and ask if this person had bought arsenic? How did one get hemlock? Vi frowned and then thought again, *Why the two poisons?*

She wasn't able to come up with an answer as she paced and then Rita returned, bringing Denny along with her and the dark-haired man. He wasn't particularly handsome, but he had a strong frame, and a clear gaze, and he took the sight of the two women in with shock.

"Margaret!" he breathed, a broken sound. "My god, Margaret!"

He was across the sick bay in a flash and then on his knees next to the other woman. She didn't move at his sob, and he actually laid his face down on her body and cried like a man who had just lost everything that mattered.

"She's not gone yet," Nanny Jane said kindly. "She is awake and asleep without being aware, but she seems to be slowly coming back to us."

He turned his gaze up and asked, "Will she?" To Vi's disgust he added, "What does it matter? We'll never be happy. We are forever thwarted."

Violet crossed the room and slapped his face. He gasped in shock and Violet told him, "Enough of that. They are going to live, and if you want to be part of that life, you will rise up like a man and fight for what matters."

"Read to her," Kate ordered. "Tell her that you love her. Make her pretty promises and then swear to yourself you'll make them come true."

Kate backed away and Nanny Jane lifted knitting that Violet hadn't noticed before and went back to work. Violet paced as he spoke to Margaret, ignoring what he said. The sight of him at Margaret's bedside had removed him from the suspect list as far as Violet was concerned. Perhaps she was wrong, but she didn't think so.

She thought back to the sight of Liam, weeping for his wife, and wondered if he also could be removed. But that didn't make sense. The problem she told herself again was the two poisons.

"Do you know what would happen if one of the sisters died? As far as this shipping business goes?" Violet asked Wenzel.

He looked up from his whispering and said, "I know nothing."

"What did Margaret tell you would happen if she left her husband?"

"She didn't." Wenzel broke into crying again. "She refused to speak of it. She said it was impossible."

"Did she admit she loved you?"

"She did."

Vi's head tilted and she asked, "What else concerned her? Outside of her fiend husband."

"A fiend indeed!" Wenzel said the words like they were the darkest of curses. "The worst of men who could hurt an angel."

Violet didn't bother to argue with him. This wasn't an angel before him, however, Margaret was a woman struggling to survive. A woman who was of *this* world and had this world's frailties. Again, Vi asked, "What else bothered her? Surely her only concern wasn't her husband?"

"She hated Oskar too," Wenzel said. "If an angel can hate, my Margaret hated Oskar even more than Liam."

"Is Oskar violent as well?"

Wenzel's face screwed up, but he shook his head. "She loves Ruth more than she loves herself, my sweet Margaret."

"Then why did she hate Oskar?" Kate asked gently, using that sweet tone and nature to pull out information that people might have held onto otherwise.

Wenzel paused. "Oskar made Ruth believe he loved her. He brought her away from everything and the moment she was secured, he went back to his whore. He broke Ruth's heart and Margaret could never forgive such a thing."

Violet turned to her own twin. They eyed each other, each believing Wenzel's story. What would they bear for the other? What pains would they set aside to see their twin happy?

"What did Margaret want for Ruth then?"

Wenzel sighed. "There was no out. Not for either of them. They had discussed it. They had tried to find out if there was a way when they went home this last time. They thought that if only their family would stand by them, they could leave their husbands and do charity work or something."

Violet didn't roll her eyes, but she wanted to. The sisters' best idea had been to throw themselves at their family, ask for forgiveness and provide lifelong penance for falling in love with the wrong men?

"What did their family say?" Kate asked, low.

"Their mother said that their father would never support them in such a scandal and to set it aside. She blamed them. Spoke to them about the lack of children and the lack of loving manners. She said to supplicate their husbands, to anticipate their needs, to be kinder and more lovely."

Rita scoffed darkly for all of the women there. "What idiocy."

"No wonder they came home hopeless." Vi returned to her pacing as she considered.

"Does anyone know if they discovered how the poisons were administered?"

Denny answered that one. "They did, but the first officer and his fellows took it into the brig. No one is talking and no one has seen Jack or Ham. Luncheon was delivered. Coffee and tea. It won't surprise me if they keep at those fellows until the day is long gone, but we won't hear a word until they let our boys free."

Vi sighed. If they could talk together about what had happened, they'd be able to weave together some of the tale, she thought. They needed Jack and Ham and their knowledge. Jack and Ham, on the other hand, needed the information Violet and the rest had discovered.

CHAPTER 12

*V*iolet heard the brig open when silence fell upon the little sick bay and they all looked up, listening for the tell-tale sign of one of their own. No such luck. Vi finally groaned and said, "I need coffee before my brain revolts. Once I have coffee, I need air."

She left and with her came Kate and Denny. Kate parted almost immediately to check on her daughters and she and Denny found a steward who sent tea to the nursery and then coffee to Vi's cabin. Vi fished through her pocket for her key and found two. Her gaze widened and she had to hide a smile as she pulled the treasure out of her pocket. Vi glanced down and then Denny followed her gaze.

"What's all this?"

"Jolly good fun," Vi whispered back, elbowing him for speaking too loudly. She winked when he gave her an askance glance and then said, "We shall have to order something else to this room."

"We've already gotten a dark look, dear Vi. I believe your steward knows that I am not your husband."

Vi glanced and saw Baldwin watching them with an expressionless face, but his eyes were condemning.

"We are being quite scandalous," Vi agreed. "For those with ill-flavored thoughts, it isn't possible for a man and a woman to be unobserved and not indulging in some sort of scandalous affair."

Baldwin blushed and Vi announced, "Mr. Baldwin, we'll have dinner in this room."

Denny squeaked, but Baldwin just said, "Very good, ma'am."

Vi laughed and then told Denny, "Are you afraid?"

"Of Jack?" Denny demanded. "Very much so. I am not a fool. He, my dear Vi, is a beast, and I am a flower."

"A delicate flower?" Vi demanded.

"Indeed. Most breakable," Denny added.

He met her gaze directly and Vi winked. She inserted one of the keys into the lock and twisted. The key refused to turn. Vi coughed and then slipped it into the pocket and tried the other key. It opened the door. The moment they entered the room, she heard Baldwin move past. Vi pushed Denny further into the room and then placed her ear next to the door. She waited, counting aloud so Denny knew what she was up to.

Once she reached one hundred, she cracked the door. Baldwin was gone. Vi winked at Denny and then tip-toed down the passage towards the small steward's compartment. It was, as she hoped, empty. Violet hurried back to the cabin assigned to the Hansons. She slipped the key into the door and glanced over her shoulder at Denny who followed her without surprise.

"I should have guessed."

"You really should have," Violet agreed. "Silly boy."

Violet pushed into the cabin and glanced around with Denny quickly closing the door behind them.

"Surely the stewards will have searched this already?"

Vi glanced at him and then asked, "Oh really? You would like to go to dinner then? Perhaps we could join in the dancing again?"

Denny shuddered. "Lila told me flatly that she would no more join in one of the Annabelle's parties than she would volunteer to do the wash for an orphanage."

Vi laughed. "Lila *is* my favorite. Can you imagine her trying to do any sort of laundry at all?"

Denny snorted as Violet began flipping through Margaret's clothes. "It so happens," Denny said seriously, "I can. She washes her own underthings and stockings."

Vi looked up in surprise. She supposed that Lila must have. Vi had done the same once. She turned from Margaret's rather normal clothes. A few evening gowns and cocktails dresses, several more day dresses, a rather pretty jumper, and one pair of sensible trousers.

There was nothing that was worthy of note. Vi pulled out the small drawer in the trunk where Margaret kept her stockings. She frowned and glanced at Denny who was looking away as though stockings were somehow quite lurid. Vi laughed at him and shoved the stockings back when she felt something that wasn't silk. Vi pulled the stockings out and found a pile of letters. She glanced through them, noting that they were love letters from the useless Wenzel Wagner.

She didn't read them, though she wanted to. Wenzel

had not been the one who poisoned Margaret. "Perhaps Ruth."

Vi's voice had been low, but Denny asked, "What now?"

Vi put the letters back and said, "I could see Wenzel having tried to poison Ruth but not Margaret."

"Why?" Denny stared at Vi as though she'd taken leave of her senses.

"He's jealous of her, I think," Vi told him. "Or at least I could *see* him being jealous of the twin."

"Jack isn't jealous of Victor," Denny told Vi easily. "Why should Wenzel be jealous of Ruth?"

Vi lifted a brow and said, "Jack isn't Wenzel."

Denny eyed Vi and asked, "Are you jealous of Kate?"

Vi paused, actually thinking it over and then said honestly, "At times, yes."

"Are you really?" Denny gasped.

"I miss the days when I could just barge into Victor's room and throw myself on his bed. I suppose, even though I wouldn't go back, I miss when Victor and I woke in the same nursery and spent the day in mischief."

"I miss those days myself," Denny said easily, and she could see that he understood. It wasn't that either of them wanted to go back. It was just that there were occasional moments of longing for the simpler times. "We shared a room so often as schoolboys. He woke up mischievous some days and then I'd know those days would be full of excitement."

Vi sighed and said, "I wonder how she could have been poisoned."

"Surely, it was in her food?"

Vi didn't object. It seemed likely enough. "We had

dinner together, in the dining room." A moment later, "But the coffee."

Vi could see it then. Someone could have poisoned the coffee that Vi had sent to the room. She was almost blinded by her fury at the idea. Her intentional kindness used to hurt the poor woman, perhaps murder her.

They searched the room more fully and Vi turned to Denny. "What do you think, my friend?"

"I don't know," he admitted. "I can never figure out things like you and Jack and Ham, Vi."

Violet sighed and said, "There's nothing here."

"Shall we leave before your Baldwin sends for Jack?"

"I suppose we should change and go to dinner," Violet muttered.

They separated in the hall and when Baldwin knocked on the door, Vi swung it wide, showing that Denny wasn't present. He looked in and then glanced at Vi. "Never mind. I'll be eating in the dining room instead."

He wasn't pleased but he simply said, "Very good."

Vi dressed without thinking about her clothes. She almost didn't pay attention to what she put on other than to see it was black. She wore black for the twins who may well have but one survive. It would be better, Violet thought, to have them both die rather than one survive. She knew it was the blue outlook that plagued her, but it wasn't as though either of them had anything other than their twin. A father who didn't protect, a mother who told them to placate, a philandering husband on the one hand, and an abusive one on the other.

Vi put on a bright red lip to go with her black dress. It was intended to be an insult to her outlook, a denial of what was happening. Her gaze was fixed inside of herself, so she didn't see Jack until she felt his touch on her arm. Vi gasped, though she knew him the moment he touched her.

"I thought you were procuring a confession."

"There is no such confession to be had. For some time now, they've both refused to speak other than to insult."

Vi examined his face. He seemed tired, and she cupped his cheek. "Have you been back to the sick bay?"

"I left for a while," Vi admitted. "Denny and I tried searching Margaret's cabin, but there is nothing there to be seen."

"She seems to be waking," Jack said. "Nanny Jane thinks she'll survive."

"Oh!" Vi grinned easily. "What wonderful news. Is Ruth any better?"

"She has sat up. She can't speak yet, but her pain is lessening. She brightened considerably when Nanny said her sister seemed better."

"Oh!" Violet wound her arm through his. "Shall we go to the cabin, have a private dinner, and go to bed early? Perhaps in the morning we can walk around the ship and take in the air?"

"Violet, darling," Jack pulled her into an offshoot of a passage that seemed to be going to a less busy side of the ship. They were able to stay in the shadows as others passed by on the way to dinner. "Liam says he will speak, if he speaks to you."

"To me?" Vi's mouth had dropped open in utter shock. "Why me?"

Jack shook his head and then admitted, "I don't think

it's you, Vi. He does *not* like me very much. Refusing to answer my questions in favor of yourself is his revenge."

Vi examined his face and asked, "Are you all right, Jack?"

"I should like to beat this Liam within an inch of his life and finish by wringing his neck."

Violet waited, but Jack seemed conflicted. She finally said, "Jack darling, we owe it to ourselves to see if we can find out what happened to these women. What if they live? What if they live and it is expected that they go home to men such as those? I can't abide that. Not if I don't do what I can."

Jack kissed her forehead. "I am entirely unsurprised."

"Am I so predictable?"

"Vi, darling." Jack rubbed the back of his neck sheepishly and then surprised them both by a laugh. "Vi, you joke that I am a knight, fighting for the weak, but it is you."

She rolled her eyes and said, "I am not talking to that man in an evening gown without dinner."

"Then shall we have some? We can eat in our cabin." Jack wasn't wearing evening clothes and she considered ordering dinner to her cabin, but remembered the look on Baldwin's face and imagined requesting dinner from him once again.

She laughed at the thought and was forced to confess what she had done. Jack listened without surprise and told her, "You'll gain a reputation, my dear."

"I believe I already have one on this ship," Vi told him easily. "You, good sir, are a man cuckolded, and I am an interfering meddler who strays."

"Interfering meddler, yes," Jack agreed. "Incurably so, but not so unkind as to break my heart."

"Never," Vi promised.

He rolled his eyes at her and she grinned unrepentantly. "I am a man besieged by a very particular devil."

CHAPTER 13

Liam Hanson was a man enraged. The only reason he didn't attack, Vi thought, is because of the stewards standing with their arms folded. The stewards had dark looks that said they had moved quite past any sympathy they might have had.

Vi took a seat opposite him. "Mr. Hanson, I wasn't very kind earlier today." She was channeling Kate, and it was quite foreign to her.

He glared at her as Vi sat across from him. "They think your wife will live."

A relieved expression crossed his face and he slumped into his chair. "Do they? I thought I had lost her."

Vi very much hoped that he had, but she said, "I can imagine that you're relieved. Hopefully we can come together now and figure out what happened to her and how to protect her again."

He examined Vi's face, but since he didn't know her,

he didn't see her disgust. Violet rubbed her brow, feeling a growing headache and asked kindly, "Have you eaten?"

He scowled and nodded. Vi glanced towards Jack and saw his expression. He was protective and unhappy she was present.

"Tell me all about it," Vi said. "Why did you go to England?"

"It's part of our arrangement with their father. When he invested in the company, he wanted us to come back and update him on the company."

For a moment there, Violet thought that the twins' father might have insisted because he wanted to see his daughters. She sighed in disappointment for the twins and then asked, "And how long was your visit?"

"A fortnight," he said. He shot her a furious glance and said, "What does that have to do with someone trying to murder my Maggie?"

Violet shrugged and pretended to be needy and a little stupid, as if she couldn't understand herself and needed help. "What little I can tell you about what I know is that they need an idea of your usual life, so they can discover where things went awry."

"Awry?" Liam Hanson snorted and Vi could tell that he was just pretending to work with her. He wanted her here, so he could rule over Jack and nothing more. Bringing in his wife and mocking her, Hanson was sure would torment Jack. Hanson couldn't imagine that Jack trusted Vi to not be disturbed. That Hanson's efforts to bother Vi would hurt no one, and in the process she might well win against him.

"Surely being poisoned isn't normal among your family?"

Hanson paused just long enough that Violet demanded, "Is it?"

He cleared his throat and said surely not.

Vi, however, was no fool, and she had seen the surprise in his face. "They'll find out when we land and then your lies will make you look worse."

"Who said I lied?"

"Your face," Vi snapped. "Your surprise and your momentary horror. Who was poisoned before?"

Hanson cleared his throat and then cursed. Jack snapped, "Enough of that."

Vi gave her husband a dark, mocking look. It wasn't as though he himself hadn't cursed in front of her before. He wasn't amused, but he said nothing.

"Who was poisoned?" Violet asked gently as though they were having a private confidence.

Liam Hanson considered not answering. Violet leaned forward and said softly, persuasively, "Mr. Hanson, it is necessary you do all that can be done to find your wife's poisoner, so she'll be safe. If this has happened before, then we do need to know."

He shrugged and then said, "One of Oskar's sisters. It is believed she poisoned herself."

Vi's head tilted and she asked, "Believed or known?"

"Who can tell?" Hanson snapped. "I have no idea. Ask Oskar."

Violet glanced at Jack who, she knew, was cataloging every passing moment. "Of course, why should you know?"

"Exactly," Hanson snapped. "Just so."

Violet said, "But you are *partners* with Oskar. How long have you known him?"

Liam wasn't pleased with the question, but it was one that could be easily verified. "Since we were boys. Our fathers, with Milly's, started the business. When it started to struggle, we looked for investors and Oskar met Ruth."

"Met and pursued Ruth?"

Liam smirked and added, "Just so."

"While loving Milly as you did."

The smirk faded and the frown was back. He said nothing. Violet's voice was soft again as she said, "What if it was Oskar who poisoned them? To get rid of his wife?"

"But why my wife?" He said it as if he were saying my auto or my piece of toast. There it was, Violet realized, there was his true feeling. He no more loved Margaret than he loved anything else. Vi had never believed that Liam Hanson *had* loved his wife, but now she could see that it was a possessive. Margaret was a piece of property to Liam—owned and nothing more.

It was easy to manipulate him more when she knew what mattered to him. "Perhaps because it was your wife."

Liam Hanson's gaze narrowed and Vi saw the stupidity in it. He saw the world only through his own view. He couldn't imagine that something wasn't concerned with him. The poisoning of someone else's sister that was somehow concerned with him. The fool! The poisoning of his own wife. It was easier to believe that it was with him than her.

"What happens," Violet started, unable to hold back the mischief, "if you and your wife die? Does the full business go to Milly's father and Oskar?"

The ruddy fury was all the answer they needed. Liam

leapt to his feet, his rage too much for him. The stewards and Jack rushed forward to protect Violet. While the stewards grabbed Liam, Jack yanked Violet into his arms. She, however, was not the one who was Liam's target. He tried to throw off the stewards, so he could get to another door.

"Who's in there?" Vi demanded. She hadn't been afraid and Jack stared down at her. He wasn't even surprised at what happened and Vi reached up and patted his cheek.

Liam was taken from the door he was trying to pass through and into another room and locked inside. As that happened, Ham stepped out of the first door. "What's going on?"

Jack revealed what Vi had discovered.

Ham's gaze narrowed on Vi and he demanded, "How did you guess about the poison?"

She shrugged.

"She discovered that and sent Liam into a rage." Jack groaned and tugged Vi closed. "You have too much courage for any man to stand."

Violet let Jack lead her from the brig and into the passageway. "Did he say anything?"

Jack frowned. Vi could see the conflict in his face. "It's the two poisons. It just doesn't make sense."

Violet hooked her arm through Jack's while they peeked in at Kate and Nanny Jane. The doctor had gone, and finally, Kate was gathering up her things to go. Wenzel Wagner hadn't left and Violet wondered just how Liam Hanson would take that news if he knew.

"How are they?" Violet asked.

"They seem to be better," Kate said, joining them in

the passageway. "Are you finished? Have you learned anything?"

"I've abandoned Ham to the fiends and am taking my wife back to our cabin. We'll walk you to yours first."

"I can get there on my own," Kate told Jack with a laugh.

"Indeed you can," Jack said, "but there's possibly a poisoner on the loose, and you are precious."

"Why would they poison me?" Kate asked, not objecting to the company again. She wound her arm through Vi's, so that she had her sister-in-law on one side and Jack on the other.

"Why would they poison those sisters?" Jack asked. "I have no idea what happened. I could see a motive for Oskar trying to kill his wife, but not Margaret. He could lose his investor in his business and everything he has. I can see a motive for Liam trying to kill Margaret if he realized she was in love with another. That relationship is fated for a bad end regardless."

"Liam, however, would lose everything if Ruth dies. It's the same for Milly. Milly, if she is a monster, has every reason to get rid of Ruth but not Margaret."

"Could it be a madman?" Kate demanded. "Perhaps there's some crazed fellow who chosen them because they're twins. Maybe he poisoned them differently to see how each reacted to the poison. Maybe they were never intended to die but used as an insane medical experiment."

Jack stared at Kate and Vi whispered, "You've been reading too many of the V.V. Twinnings novels."

Kate laughed. "It makes as much sense as anything else."

"Which means, of course," Jack countered, "that none of this makes sense."

His gaze moved to Vi, and she could see him weighing the idea that *she* also was a twin. She expected the reaction the moment that Kate explained her theory. Vi didn't even think that Kate had been serious, but Jack never took Vi's safety as anything other than his first priority.

"I'm not an identical twin," Vi said before he could think about locking her in the cabin or putting her in a lifeboat and rowing her to safety.

"You *are* a twin though," Kate told Violet. "I'm not saying my theory isn't mad, but you *and Victor* need to be especially careful."

Their gazes met and Vi realized the next step the moment Kate did.

"And the babies," Vi whispered. It had been ridiculous when it was applied just to the other twins and more ridiculous when they applied it to Victor and Violet. It was, however, far less humorous when one was considering baby Vivi and Agatha.

Kate let go of Vi's arm and then they both knocked on the door of the nursery. "Is all well?" Kate asked.

"The babies are sleeping," Nanny Poppy replied. She glanced over her shoulder and said, "As is Victor."

Kate stepped into the nursery cabin followed by Violet. Jack remained in the doorway since the cabin was already crowded. Kate crossed to Victor and whispered her theory. Vi watched her brother reject the idea until his gaze landed on the babies.

A moment later he said, "We'd be stupid not to be careful."

"That goes for all of you," Jack told Victor and Violet. Vi didn't even narrow her gaze on him, roll her eyes, and scoff.

"Bloody hell," Victor groaned.

"We order nothing to our cabins. Let's just have that go for all of us," Jack told them. "We eat in the dining room. The ship arrives soon. We have but a few days to get through."

Vi would have objected save for the twins.

"The babies are going with us," Victor told Nanny Poppy. "Take Lily to Denny and Lila and tell them the concern."

"I think you're overreacting."

"It's not worth the risk," Kate told the nanny. She didn't object, but how could she?

Violet groaned a moment later. "This means we have to go to the dining room for coffee."

"And to watch our waiters as though they're all criminals," Victor stretched his neck.

"Let's just take other people's food," Kate said.

They all stared at her.

"I know it's mad," Kate said. "I know we'll be gossiped over, but who cares? Someone else orders food, we just take it from the waiter before it gets delivered. What can they do once we have it?"

Victor snorted with a laugh and said, "Darling Kate, I have never loved you more."

"And thus it begins," Denny said, rubbing his hands together with glee. He entered the dining room with a lightness to his step that declared he would never experience anything better than what was about to occur.

Lila followed after with her baby in her arms. Little Lily watched the world with interest and laughed when her father laughed. Their matching giggles were enough to have smiles sent their way. It was quite unusual for babies to be brought into the dining room and until Lily giggled with her father, most of the looks they received were disturbed.

"You do it," Violet told Jack.

He stared at her and then crossed to the waiter a few tables from them. "Excuse me?"

The waiter looked up and Jack removed the tray from the man's hands. "Sir?"

"Thank you," Jack said easily, carrying the loaded tray on his hand as though he were born to be a waiter.

Denny gasped with such delight, Vi laughed.

Jack led the way, not to their assigned table but one that hadn't been taken yet. They sat and Vi told him, "You sir, are the most excellent of providers."

Denny seated Vi and Lila. The second she was comfortable, she reached for the coffee cup that had been turned upside down, waiting for whoever this seat belonged to. Vi flipped it and held up her cup for coffee, ignoring the stares from other diners. Jack poured her coffee while another waiter approached.

"This is not your table sir."

"It is now," Jack told him, taking a seat and pouring himself coffee.

"It's so pale," Vi muttered.

"It's regular coffee," Jack told her.

She sipped and then scowled. "But I need Turkish coffee."

"Not today," Jack told her.

"I'll never survive like this."

The first waiter approached as Jack poured the last of the coffee. Jack handed over the carafe and then met the man's gaze when he didn't leave. "Yes?"

"What can I get you, sir?" The fellow stammered a little and his gaze was moving around the table as though they were mad. He had yet to see how mad they would get, Vi thought almost sympathetically.

It seemed that this waiter had decided to serve them and get rid of them rather than argue.

"We'll forage," Denny told the man. "Go about your business."

The waiter frowned, waiting for an explanation. A moment later, Denny rose. "It's my turn. It's me who is giddy as a schoolgirl now."

His high-pitched giggle drew attention and they all watched him approach the doors where the waiters entered the dining room from the kitchens. Denny watched several go by before one that he liked came out.

The waiter stood next to their table as one of his fellows rolled a loaded cart out of the kitchens. Denny stopped the man, held up a hand, and leaned in. Whatever Denny whispered had the waiter objecting, but slowly letting go of the cart.

Their waiter asked, "What is going on?"

Denny took the cart and rolled it away from the table of waiting passengers. He was overtly grinning as one of the men called, "I say, man. What the devil?"

Denny waved off the question as though he were the queen greeting her subjects. He reached their table and the waiter who was assigned to it said, "What is happening?"

"Speak with your captain," Jack told him with a firmness that lent weight to that out and out humbug.

Vi glanced at Jack and he shook his head slightly. None of them had explained their plan to the captain, but it gave the waiter enough of a pause that Denny was able to lift the dome off one of the trays.

"I believe we have ebelskivers here."

"Ooh me," Lila said. "Dare I hope for lemon curd?"

"You dare," Denny told his wife.

The next tray was kedgeree, roasted potatoes, and bacon. Denny crowed and put it in his place without regret or apology. He uncovered another tray and found an even more loaded plate of eggs, bacon, sausages and tomatoes.

Denny handed it to Jack with the expression of a man who had been robbed. The tray after that was toast and fruit and Vi was the one who reached out with happiness. She took that plate and then stole a piece of Jack's bacon and all of his roasted tomatoes. There were three more trays and when Ham and Rita arrived they were taken up too.

"What about Victor and Kate?" Vi asked, worried for her brother.

"Victor pulled the same trick as Denny here to some fellow who had ordered food to his cabin. Kate had been called to the sick bay, so he and the babies were eating together." Ham's explanation relieved Vi's mind and then she paused in her breakfast, daring to look up and around the dining room. They were being watched as though they were lions at the zoo.

Vi's gaze met Rita's, and they both burst into giggles. Baby Lily immediately joined them. Lila's lazy laugh and Denny's giddy one followed.

Ham shook his head at the two of them and looked at Jack. "These precautions are ridiculous."

"Agreed," Jack said easily.

"But so fun," Denny countered. "The only thing that could make this trip better is chalkboards."

"No," Vi said. "The next thing we know you'll be designing a special trunk like Victor with his desire to bring along a bar."

Denny stared at Vi as though she were brilliant, and she groaned.

"You did that to yourself, my love," Rita told Vi.

"Foolish girl. These random asides of yours get us into more trouble."

~

KATE ENTERED the dining room when Vi was halfway through her tomatoes. She took a seat and then begged, "Does anyone have tea?"

"We might as well," Vi answered, handing over her pale swill.

"They're both awake," Kate said after a long swallow. "They're awake, and they'll recover."

"Fully?" Jack demanded.

Kate shook her head and said, "We have no idea. The doctor is drunk within an inch of his life. Nanny Jane thinks that there could be some long-lasting effects, but death won't be one of them."

"Who knows?"

"Only Nanny. She made Wenzel leave when he started quoting poetry last night. When he objected, Nanny had him dragged from the sick bay like a robber. She told Margaret Hanson when she woke that her lover had been sent out and that she should think long and hard about whether she wanted to leave her fiend of a husband for a fool of a lover."

"She didn't," Denny breathed. "And we missed it."

"But she missed seeing you steal breakfast," Violet told Denny.

Jack handed Kate the last covered tray and said, "Good luck."

The cover was pulled back and Kate revealed a full English breakfast that had gone cold. Kate shrugged and put the cold egg on the toast along with the roasted tomatoes.

"It occurs to me," Kate said as she sipped Vi's rejected coffee, "that we haven't done our usual conversation about motives and the like. I think we should."

"Before we go see the twins?"

Kate nodded. "They might not know anything, or they might have a good idea. Since we don't know what the motive is, we don't know if they'd lie for the person they suspect."

"Speaking of motives," Rita said idly, "what are the usual ones?"

"Love," Denny shot out.

"Money," Lila added lazily.

"Hatred, jealousy," Jack added.

"With poison," Violet added, "it's called the women's weapon. So perhaps to do something that a woman can't normally do for herself."

"If we were to take love," Rita said, "we would think well, Liam maybe out of fury that he might be losing his wife."

"She did have love letters," Violet agreed. "If he discovered those, it might have been enough to drive him to murder."

Jack's expression said he wouldn't be surprised by such a thing. Except….

"Except that doesn't apply to Ruth," Ham said, repeating the problem they'd encountered time and again. "The conundrum isn't who doesn't have a motive, but who has a motive for both women."

"What if we looked at the timeline instead?" Denny's mouth was half-full of food and he was holding one hand out to his daughter, so she could grasp his forefinger. He was shaking his head even as Jack countered.

"That doesn't matter with poison. Probably, Margaret was poisoned through the unattended coffee tray. It seems likely that it was placed in the sugar. The captain put some of the food out for the ship's rats and the one who ate the sugar didn't survive."

Vi scrunched her nose, grateful to have not been part of that. She hated to think of rats on the ship at all and turned her mind away from the idea.

"And with Ruth?"

"The tooth powder."

Vi started to ask a question, but she was sidetracked by the sight of Mr. Baldwin coming into the dining room, heading towards their normal table and then stopping partway there. He turned to leave and caught sight of them. He frowned a moment, staring in confusion at where they were and at their empty table and then shook it off.

"The captain wants to see you sirs," Mr. Baldwin said to Jack and Ham.

"We'll be happy to see him when we're finished here."

Mr. Baldwin wanted to object, but he paused long enough to think better of it and leave.

Ham listed the names once again. "Milly Kristiansen has motive to kill Ruth but not Margaret. In fact, like Oskar, she has every reason to want Margaret to survive. Liam has a reason to kill Margaret but not Ruth. The only one who has a motive to kill both is Wenzel Wagner, and that's only if you give him the weakest of motives. I don't buy it."

Vi hadn't asked about Oskar the night before. Not

when her mind was encompassed with the babies.

"What about the dead sister?"

"I asked him about that," Ham said. "He admitted that his sister had been killed by poison, *but* he said it was self-administered. She had been quite unhappy, she used her own sleeping pills, and she left a note. Both he and Ruth had been out of the country at the time. He even alibied Liam."

"He did?" Vi demanded.

"He did. He said that Liam had also been away. He said, in fact, that he'd love it if Liam had murdered Anya and ruined himself, but Liam had not even been there. It seems that Oskar's sister had left home with her sleeping pills, gone to visit a supposed school friend, but it had all been a lie. It was in her note. She wanted to avoid her mother finding her body. She had gone to stay at a convent for a few days. There were no men there. She took her pills and left the convent, laying herself down in the unconsecrated graves with her note in her hand. There was never any doubt about what happened and who was responsible."

"Bloody hell," Denny breathed.

As a group they had imagined it all; it was too easy not to picture something so dramatic.

"Why did Liam make it seem as though there was a question?" Vi snapped.

"He's a fool and self-encompassed. I asked Oskar just that," Ham told them. "He laughed and said Liam could make anything about him."

"None of this makes sense," Violet snapped. "This case is…is…"

"Stupid," Denny finished and no one disagreed.

CHAPTER 15

*J*ust outside of the sick bay, the first mate stood with the doctor. The second man was sniffling as though he had gotten ill, but Vi suspected it was another round of needing alcohol and not getting it. She was sympathetic to an extent. She enjoyed drinks fairly regularly but had never done so with the idea that at some point she would start *needing* them. He should not, however, put others at risk because of his needs. Thank goodness for Nanny Jane, because the doctor wouldn't have been able to put the IV in the twin sisters.

"What's this I hear about your odd behavior?" the first mate asked.

"It occurred to us," Jack said low, "that it was possible the sisters were attacked simply because they're twins. We have two sets among us."

The first mate frowned, not bothering to hide his doubt. "And you consider this a real concern?"

"No," Jack said flatly. "I think we don't have enough information about why those sisters were attacked, and we need more details in order to discover who might want to get rid of both of them."

"Then why are you behaving this way?"

"It's not worth the risk," Jack told the first mate without regret. "I think we have a very small chance of danger and in saying that, the danger extends primarily to my wife, her twin brother, and her nieces who aren't even walking yet. I won't attend a pair of baby funerals when all I have to do is be a little ridiculous."

The first mate rocked back on his heels, considering. "Let's see if we can end this now that they're awake. I don't like you, Wakefield. But, it would be best if we could solve this aboard."

"Of course it would be," Jack offered consolingly. "If we don't, the suspects could disperse and someone would be able to get away with quite a horrible crime."

"You know," Violet said, thinking something that made her shiver, "if one were a madman, striking on steamships or railways may well be the best way to get away with the crime."

The first mate snorted, giving Violet that look that said she was a silly woman, when Jack said, "If the criminal were clever enough to attack that way, it would be almost impossible to find them. No motive but madness. If he was careful to have no witnesses, there would be nothing to link him to the crime. The madman would win every time. If he were very, very careful and changed how and through what avenue his attacks occurred, the police might not even realize that they had a madman on their hands."

The first mate glanced between the two of them with his jaw dropped. Violet laughed at the look on the man's face and said to Jack, "Enough! We'll be the suspects in another moment."

"Why are you here, ma'am?" The tone was respectful enough, but only just.

Jack clapped the first mate on his back. "We have two women who have been assaulted and are afraid. Violet will provide a measure of comfort."

Vi kept her expression even and her eyes wide and innocent.

The first mate paused and then nodded. "The husbands are quite upset. We need to discover what happened and let them out. Hanson is demanding to see his wife. Nielsen is demanding to see his lover."

"We should do that," Vi said. "And watch." She paused for a long minute and said, "Well, maybe not for poor Margaret. Surely it can't be good for her recovery to have her husband looming over her."

"We would be there," the first mate said.

Vi frowned at him, noting the lack of sympathy and guessed the fellow didn't care so much about Margaret's continual abuse. He noticed Vi's look and lifted a brow. Yes, she thought, Vi didn't like him at all.

"She needs to stay out of the room."

"No," Jack told the first mate, having caught the expression he sent towards Vi. "We need all the help we can get to solve this mystery. We only have today before the ship arrives."

"I said no," the first mate told Jack.

Jack paused and eyed the first mate, who stared back

in challenge. Vi rolled her eyes, which the first mate caught.

"Do you have a problem with that, ma'am?"

Vi placed her hand on Jack's arm as she felt him tense.

"Your captain put Ham and I in charge of this investigation due to our time as detectives for Scotland Yard. Has that changed?" Jack's cool tone sounded almost bored, but Vi could feel the steel of his frame.

The first mate's reply was only, "Not yet."

"Then step aside and be quiet." Jack took Vi's arm and pulled her with him into the sick bay. "Just be yourself, Vi. You ask the questions. They'll feel more comfortable with you."

That was said for the first mate who snorted again. Vi winked at both of them because she knew it would irritate the first mate. She waited until he reacted and then turned away, putting him out of her mind. She gasped in delight as she saw the twins sitting up, side-by-side. They'd moved onto the same hospital bed and Kate was helping Ruth to drink from a teacup.

"You look fabulous," Vi said, approaching to squeeze Ruth's hand and then reaching over to do the same to Margaret.

"Miss Jane and Mrs. Carlyle say that you found us," Margaret said. "That we survived because of you."

"I think you survived because you're fighters," Violet told them both. "Are you ready to continue the fight?"

The first mate snorted and Vi tried to hide her disgust. Margaret didn't even seem to notice the derision, but Ruth wasn't impressed. Jack moved and whatever he did had Margaret tensing though Ruth had the opposite reaction and relaxed.

"I don't know what we can tell you," Ruth stuttered out. Her body was still processing the hemlock poisoning and Vi had to wonder if Ruth would ever be able to speak easily again.

"How about, do you know who poisoned you?" Vi asked.

They both shook their heads. Margaret reached out and took Ruth's hand.

"The biggest problem we're having," Violet said gently, "is that there are motives for someone to murder one of you but not both of you. Is there anyone who would benefit from having you both die?"

Both sisters shook their heads again. They didn't even need to consult. Vi leaned back. Their greatest hope had been that the sisters would be able to provide some illumination as to why they were poisoned.

"No threats?"

Shaking heads.

"No enemies?"

"No," Margaret whispered. "Not for both of us."

Violet sighed and asked, "If we can't find out what happened to you, what will you do?"

"We're going home to England," Ruth struggled to say. "Father has sent a wireless."

Vi sighed with relief. The sisters had every chance to survive now. Their hands were clasped and there was a sense of relief.

"Your husbands are demanding to see you."

Margaret flinched but Ruth rolled her eyes. Vi met Ruth's gaze and Ruth seemed to be trying to lift her brow.

Vi laughed and said, "All right. The truth is, the obsessive Liam is demanding to see Margaret. However, Oskar demanded to see his mistress."

Ruth didn't even react. She just stared blankly at Vi and then nodded.

"He's a beast!" Margaret told her twin. "He never deserved you."

"He l-l-l-lied for F-f-f-father's m-m-money." Her emotions were heightened and it was more difficult for her to speak.

Violet held back a sigh. She had hoped that Ruth would reveal some reason why her husband might have tried to kill them both. Only, she was just confirming the same conclusion the rest of them had come to.

Violet glanced at Jack and he nodded to the first mate who left and returned with Oskar Nielsen.

"Ruth, darling," Oskar said, his gaze moving over his wife, "thank God you're fine."

"You wouldn't have minded if she died," Margaret shot out.

"Oh, the silent one speaks," Oskar snapped. He glanced at his audience and said, "I'm sorry, Margaret, it's been a difficult few days. They're keeping me in the brig and I'm on edge. I'm glad both of you survived."

Violet watched them like a hawk. You could almost see the old hatreds in the air. This wasn't a family who supported and loved each other, but Vi hadn't expected that fairy tale. Oskar spoke with them for a while and then Ruth said, "Father is coming to Norway to take Margaret and me home."

"What?" Oskar demanded. "No."

"Yes," Ruth stammered.

Margaret reached out for her sister's hand and spoke for both of them. "Someone tried to kill us."

"We have vows!" Oskar snapped.

"Which you've broken," Margaret shot back. She was trembling, but she spoke up for her sister. "We're leaving, and you can't stand in our way."

"I can! She's my wife."

"You won't win. Not when Father steps in."

Oskar leaned back and Violet had a sudden idea that the true ruler in this situation was the distant father of the twins.

"Perhaps the best thing you can do," Violet inserted to see what he would say, "is to negotiate with your wife before her father arrives, so she can speak on your behalf."

"Negotiate?" Oskar growled. "She's *my* wife."

"And," Violet told him flatly, "that's *her* father, and *her* father's money. You have freedom to offer, and she has the potential ability to persuade her father not to abandon you entirely."

Oskar did not like that, but Violet told him, "She wants freedom, a generous allowance, and for you to leave her alone."

"An allowance!"

"Or," Violet told him flatly, "she'll tell her father *everything.*"

Vi had no idea what that meant, but she guessed that Oskar was up to more than just having a lover. It was a wild accusation based upon instinct, but the thing with generalities is that Oskar knew what he had been doing. He knew the worst of it, and it was that horror that was careening around his head.

Oskar's fury was high and Violet told him, "They don't have anything to lose, Mr. Nielsen. It's their very lives at risk. You're past pleading and negotiations. This failed murder makes any situation where they're able to live a better one."

He met Vi's gaze and she lifted a brow, forcing him to see his wife's point of view.

"She's right," Jack told Oskar. "You should consider it. If they go home to their father, get the divorce that is almost inevitable, given that we *all* know you have been unfaithful and there is a clear argument to be made that you could have been the poisoner, the divorce would be granted."

Oskar slammed back and said, "I did not try to kill my wife or her whining sister."

"That *is* what any murderer would say," Violet inserted.

"I might let Ruth go," Oskar said, and he grinned meanly, "but Liam will never let Margaret go."

Vi lifted a brow and told him, "Why don't you leave that to us." She had *no* idea how they were going to make that happen, but Oskar didn't need to know that.

He snorted meanly and Vi glanced at Jack.

"The investigation is not complete. You are the most likely suspect."

"You can't keep me locked up. I have rights."

"You have the rights the captain allows you while at sea," Jack told him. "For now, the captain prefers to keep you locked up."

iam Hanson swaggered into the sick bay like a man who had come to take his place in the world. The moment he entered, Margaret folded in on herself and Ruth sat forward, almost blocking her sister from her husband.

"Maggie!" He rushed forward and Maggie flinched. A look of rage crossed his face and Violet found herself flinching along with his wife.

"That's far enough," Jack told Hanson. "You didn't want shackles, but you'll get them."

The rage intensified, but Liam held himself back.

"Maggie, what has happened to you?"

"You poisoned her," Ruth said. She didn't stutter that time and Violet thought that it was a twin's fierce love that gave her the strength to speak.

"I didn't! I would never."

"You have been one wild punch from killing her for

years," Ruth said. She struggled to speak that time. "You're a monster."

Liam Hanson stared at his sister-in-law with such clear hatred Violet thought suddenly that this man could have murdered his wife and his sister-in-law. His expression adjusted when it landed on Margaret. There was something mad in that gaze, something that was horrible, but Vi—she just wasn't sure that Liam had decided to kill his wife. Did he know about her lover?

Violet frowned and then did something she wasn't very proud of. "Perhaps he did try to kill Margaret."

"Not my Maggie," Liam said fiercely. "Not my soft little angel."

"I'm only surprised that you went for her and her twin, but not the lover. Perhaps you tried for Wagner and failed?"

The monstrous change in Liam's expression and Margaret's low wail told Violet that he hadn't known. He lunged for his wife, but the steward who was just behind him wrestled Hanson to the ground. He was bestial in his fight, but Jack must have chosen the steward for his abilities. With a trip, a hard jab to the kidneys, and an arm around Hanson's neck, he was debilitated.

"Wagner? Ruth's milksop?" His voice was hoarse due to the elbow at his throat.

Violet didn't answer. Her gaze was fixed on Margaret who curled into her twin, too scared to cry. Ruth's expression had shifted to fierce. Each twin seemed better able to fight for the other than themselves.

"I'll kill you," Liam shouted. "You and Wagner."

Vi shot a look to Jack who helped haul Hanson to his feet and drag him from the sick bay.

"I doubt a stiff drink is good for you right now," Violet told the sisters, "but I could go for one. Your husband is terrifying."

Margaret didn't look up from her sister's shoulder and Vi shook her head. She rubbed her brow and dropped down next to the twins. They had wrapped each other up in tight hugs and Violet didn't doubt for a moment how much they needed the other. There was something about the person you had known from your very first moments. A shared womb, a shared life, a relationship that started with your first breath and was forever wound together.

Vi, of course, couldn't help but think of her own twin. Violet rose, ignoring the first mate and the doctor who watched her as though she was the enemy. She straightened the sick bay absently while she thought. In between lining up bottles, and folding the extra blanket at the end of the bed, Violet fiddled with her wedding ring and paced.

"You two," Violet said, frustrated. "It's like we have two killers, but what are the chances?"

Ruth started and Margaret gasped low. Suddenly Violet was very sure that those women knew *exactly* who had poisoned them. She glanced at the first mate and the doctor who had blindly noticed nothing and then to Kate who had caught the same reaction that Violet had.

Why? Violet looked at the first mate and said charmingly, "We need a hero."

He rolled his eyes, but Violet didn't think he'd avoid answering her call. Her mind raced. She said it before she'd thought of an errand. Her gaze moved to Kate with wide eyes and her sister-in-law understood immediately.

"It's more for me," Kate admitted. The man didn't even notice that neither of the women had a chance to confer. "I need my husband."

Kate made her voice quaver and put one hand on her stomach where the baby was growing and the first mate's gaze widened in horror. He nodded and rushed from the room and Violet glanced back to the twins.

To the doctor, Vi said, "There's quite a large bottle of bourbon in my cabin." She listed the cabin number and tossed the man her key.

When he was gone, Kate said, "He's going to steal your jewels."

"Jack locked them up." Violet turned her attention to the twins and examined them. Neither would meet her gaze. "You gave yourselves away."

Margaret moaned low and Ruth's jaw firmed. They didn't speak.

"You know who poisoned you."

The twin sisters looked at each other and then back to Violet.

"Nanny, have they spoken to each other about the crime?"

She shook her head. "I agree with you, however. They've talked about how the other feels and surviving and going home, but not about who tried to kill them."

"You know what's interesting?" Violet said idly as though they were discussing the fine weather outside. "I am a twin myself."

"So?"

"So, I know about that half-speak. That language that only the other can understand. I know about how you can convey a thousand things with a look. How a hand squeeze translates to an entire essay with any other person. You didn't talk about it, but you did."

Margaret shook her head, but Ruth met Vi's gaze. "That isn't something you can prove."

Why? Violet asked herself, staring at them, would they protect the poisoner? What could they possibly gain from such an action? She saw them turn and look at each other. She saw that *something* she had done herself a thousand times before. She'd never seen it from the outside, never seen another set of twins speak without speaking and leave her out. She felt suddenly sorry for the many times she'd done it to her friends.

Why would anyone kill both of them? Why were they protecting the murderer? As far as Vi could see they only cared about the other. The husbands were both useless and horrible. Milly Kristiansen was no friend of theirs. Maybe, *maybe*, they cared about Wenzel Wagner, but they wouldn't protect him. Ruth would stand up and protect Margaret even from Wenzel. Vi had seen Ruth do what she could for her sister already.

Margaret, the weaker one, still tried to protect Ruth when her philandering husband had come in careless and pretending.

Vi's jaw almost dropped as another idea occurred to her. "Do they know how you were poisoned?"

Margaret paused and then said, "All I had that day was the coffee you had ordered for me. I didn't answer the steward's knock when it arrived since I don't care for coffee normally, but I was light headed, so I poured a cup and sipped at it. Turkish coffee is quite awful isn't it?"

No, Vi thought, it was the nectar of the gods, but she

didn't say anything and Margaret nervously filled the silence.

"I drank some that day and the coffee must have hid the taste of the poison."

Oh, Vi thought, oh it added up. She turned to Ruth and asked, "And you?"

"I hadn't eaten, but Mr. Hamilton said that I might have been poisoned through my tooth powder."

"Your tooth powder?"

Ruth nodded, taking her sister's hand and squeezing comfortingly.

Vi frowned and then asked, "How odd. I suppose it was a new tooth powder?"

Ruth paused and then asked carefully, "However did you know?"

Vi glanced at Kate and at Nanny Jane and then answered, "Well how else would such a mistake be made?"

Ruth frowned and said, "You don't think my poisoning was purposeful?"

"I don't think you were the intended victim."

Ruth laughed nervously and the idea was cementing itself into certainty in Vi's head. She bit down on her bottom lip and said, "You must have been quite horrified when your husband's sister took her life."

"Of course I was," Ruth said. "How could I not be?"

"Did you discuss it often with your sister? Missing the cues of your sister-in-law's imminent demise?"

"Well, of course we did," Margaret said. "What does it matter?"

"You don't like sugar in your coffee, do you?"

"I don't like sweet in general," Margaret replied. "Liam—" She shook her head.

"You are *not* fat." Vi snapped, guessing that Margaret's carefulness in what she ate had more to do with her husband's insults.

"Regardless, I rarely indulge," Margaret told them.

"But the Turkish coffee was so strong, especially since you don't normally like coffee. You must have put quite a bit of sugar in when you normally didn't."

Margaret nodded. There was a dawning fear in her eyes as she met Violet's gaze. There was a silent plea there. Stop, it said, please stop.

Vi considered. It would be so easy to just stop. To not say what she'd realized. What was the sentence for attempted murder in Norway? Especially when you got the wrong victim? When you accidentally got a sister who never indulged in sugar rather than the husband who probably always did? What was the sentence when you tried to kill your sister's husband and she tried to kill yours? When a united horror of a poisoning and a united life led each sister to the same escape for their beloved.

Why had they been unable to find the person who would kill them both? Because there wasn't one. There were two killers in the group and they'd both failed rather horribly. Why had these sisters not discussed who had poisoned them? Because they had figured it out in moments. Because they might have even discussed it here and there. Because they had separately decided to act on the behalf of the other.

Vi didn't even blame them. She watched them and *knew,* and they watched her and knew exactly what she was thinking. Vi looked at Kate, who had guessed that something was afoot. Had she put the pieces together as well?

Before Violet could ask or say anything, she turned and found Jack. He had entered the room and he, too, knew that Violet had figured out what had happened. She and her husband were not on the level of silent communication of herself and Victor, but the problem with Jack is that he knew her so well, and he was just so damn perceptive.

Violet was an unrepentant meddler. She was also one who didn't always speak up when she knew what had happened. She had even told a woman what to say to get out of a murder. It was that, she thought, that gave her away and then gave the twins away. Who would Violet protect? Only them.

Jack turned his considering gaze to the two women and said, "It always was a problem. Two poisons, two victims, no one with overlapping motives."

Margaret let out a low moan. Ruth asked, "S-s-s-so? W-what d-d-does that have to do with us?"

Ignorance was the perfect defense. A crime committed at sea. No deaths. Violet realized that unless they confessed the sisters would never be caught. They might even get what they wanted in the end—a safer, happier twin.

When Violet finished explaining her theory, her audience stared in shock. Jack was the only who hadn't been caught by surprise.

"Bloody hell," Denny said. "Why did I have to miss it?"

"Sick bays equal bedpans, my lad," Lila told her husband.

"How do we get them to confess?" Ham asked.

His wife answered, "We don't."

Ham looked at Rita and then at the rest of the group. They all had varying degrees of support and repulsion. Victor was the one who summed it up. "I don't think I care to spend my time further with this matter."

"I would murder someone who was beating you," Violet told him. "As your twin, it's my responsibility to save you from those who hurt you."

Vi didn't blame the sisters. That is what it came down to. She just didn't care to help further.

"I don't endorse poisoning," Rita told her husband. She paused and then her head tilted as she slowly added, "Or murder."

"Or attempted murder," Vi agreed. She was somewhat sick about the whole affair. It was too easy to see why the women had acted as they had. It was too easy to sympathize with would-be killers and that made her feel quite disgusted with herself. "I hate this."

"But I think we're out of it."

"I don't know," Denny said, "I was looking forward to dinner."

Violet laughed and said, "I can just see you in your evening clothes."

"They've probably come up with a plan of action."

"Which is something that we need to do," Ham said, looking at the others. "Are we really going to just…do nothing?"

"They're not stupid," Jack told Ham. "I don't like this either. I should like to see them somehow pay. A convent even. But—we can't make them confess, and to be honest, we can't even call in the Yard and to hunt down who bought the poison."

"They're not stupid," Vi repeated. "I would sincerely doubt that Ruth Nielsen purchased poison. Especially something like arsenic which isn't all that hard to find if you want to."

"Hemlock is," Ham said.

"It also grows naturally if you know what to look for," Violet added. "It's not like we can interview the squirrels. I did ask and I guess that Liam Hanson allows his wife rambles for the exercise."

Kate shifted and they could all see the anger in her

face. She explained, "To keep that trim figure for his abuse."

"Probably untraceable poisons. No death." Ham cursed. "We really can't catch them, can we?"

"I don't think so," Jack answered. "It seems they were rather more careful in the murder plans than their wedding plans."

"They probably learned to be precise after such a mistake." Lila yawned and then said, "I think that means we can order coffee again, and I need it."

"Hear, hear," Victor said. "My head is pounding. I fear we've become quite dependent."

Jack and Ham sighed and Violet echoed it. She didn't want to be the woman who let murderers go. Perhaps they should tell the police in Norway their suspicions, but she decided to leave it to Jack and Ham. Instead, she followed her twin to the dining room for coffee and drank it in silence.

"I'd murder for you," Victor told her. "That's my problem. I would have preferred that those sisters just leave their husbands, but I can see why they didn't."

Violet didn't answer. Her head was pounding and her heart was grey and her frustration was with more than just that moment; it was with a world that made it hard for Margaret Hanson to leave the husband who left her bruised and almost broken. That left the women dependent on a father who wouldn't help them, on husbands who didn't care about them, but no. She frowned. Those sisters might not have been able to carry on with their current lifestyle without their spouses, but there *were* options.

Violet sighed, "They're going to get what they want in the end."

Her brother met her gaze and he finally shrugged. "We can't cure all the world's ills, and this is a lesser one in the grand scheme of things."

"I just worry that murder is seeming to be a reasonable choice," Violet admitted. "We have encountered too many to have innocent hearts or minds anymore. It's like Margaret and Ruth—one of the reasons they turned to poison was because it had been something they had seen before. It had been an out for another in their lives. It had become an option, horrible as it was."

"We're not killers, Vi. We don't have to be. We have each other."

Violet leaned back and closed her eyes, sipping her coffee slowly. The day passed slowly and she ended it by spending much of it near the sea, thinking about how the waves were all connected. Jack sat down next to her and said, "Ham and I tried for a confession."

"You failed?"

He nodded.

"What are you going to do?"

"Ham is doing it now."

"What?"

"He's writing a report that lists every person involved, their possible motives, and suggests how it might have been done. He's going to give it to the captain and excuse ourselves."

Violet nodded. "Are we bad people?"

His answer was slow, and she was afraid he was going to say they were. Instead what he said was, "I think there's a reason we just have to trust some things will balance out in the end. We trust that God will judge, Vi. I think we need that because it *is* complicated. Murder is wrong. I won't pretend otherwise, but so is what Hanson and Nielsen are doing to those women. One wrong doesn't justify another wrong, but there comes a point where we need a higher judge."

"And if there is no God?" Vi asked.

"Then we'll be dead and it won't matter."

They stared at each other and Vi said, "I should like to believe that there is a God. That there will be a judgement, justice, and mercy in the end. I should like to believe that our choices matter."

Jack took her hand, kissing the back of it, and said, "I should like to believe that there is the possibility for our love to last beyond our short years here. I will be the best man in this life for that day, Vi. The rest I'm handing over to whatever comes next."

They didn't speak for a long time after that and when the ship landed, Vi saw the captain and a local detective mocking Jack and Ham's report. They might be quite respected investigators in England, but it seemed that Norway was not England. The twin sisters left the ship, entered a hotel, and would soon be returning to England.

Their negotiation had ended and they would have an allowance to survive in England without their husbands, who would have the continued support of the twins' father as long as he agreed, but it seemed that as long as their lives weren't sullied with divorce, no one believed he would object.

Margaret Hanson was expected to make a full recovery, physically at least. Ruth Nielsen would have issues from the damage caused by the hemlock, but they would both live. Alive, free, and forced to carry with them what they had done.

Violet watched the twins sit, side-by-side, and hoped there would be happiness someday for them. They were in the lobby of the same hotel and Violet was grateful to be checking out. They would go out for breakfast and then onto wherever it was that Ham had planned.

With her brother, Violet asked, "Did we do the right thing?"

"We did what we could," he told her. "Our failure to get a confession doesn't put their crime on us."

"Maybe we didn't try hard enough," Violet suggested, as Jack directed a porter to gather their trunks and bring them to the front of the hotel. They were being carted to some place farther north.

"We did what we could."

"Did we?"

Vi wondered if she had handled things better if they could have trapped the twins into a confession. She wondered if she hadn't tried hard enough because she might have done the same as they had done if she were in their situation. If she hadn't thought like the would-be killers and instead thought like the hand of justice, would she have been able to get a confession? She asked her brother just that.

"What we do matters," Victor told her. "Who we love matters as well as how fiercely we love. You were thinking with empathy and love, and I think that matters more than trying to be the blind axe of justice."

"I would rather be what you just described," she told him. "I would rather be empathetic and full of love."

She hooked her arm through her twin's and laid her head against his shoulder. How lucky she was that it was *he* who was her twin rather than one of those two. She laid her head against his shoulder and asked him, "Are you happy?"

He nodded.

"Are you really?"

"Vi," Victor told her easily. "I have the right twin, the right wife, the right friends, a righteous amount of money, and perfect daughters. I am blessed to an excess. So are you."

Her gaze moved around the hotel lobby. Lila, Denny and baby Lily all snuggled together on a sofa near the window. The two nannies sat happily talking as they looked out at the street. Rita and Ham stood with Jack as he arranged the next leg of their trip. Kate had a twin in each arm and let an elderly couple coo and cluck at the babies.

"So I am," Vi agreed and felt the dawning light of happiness. They had done what they could with what they were given. It was all they could do and it was enough.

The End

HULLO FRIENDS! I am so grateful you dove in and read the latest Vi and friends mystery. If you wouldn't mind, I would be so grateful for a review.

. . .

THE SEQUEL to this book is available for preorder.

August 1926

Jack and Ham are pulled into their first solo case when a priceless treasure is stolen from Ham's home and a body is left behind. As the case progresses, Vi and Rita dive in, and somehow it becomes a competition.

Order your copy here.

A NEW SERIES is also now available for preorder at a special price.

October 1925

Severine DuNoir was twelve when she discovered the bodies of her parents, and the day after the funeral, she was sent to a convent in another country. By the time she resolves to go home, her sole focus is to reveal what happened to her parents.

Coming home, however, unveils a far more sinister plot than she could have expected. It's clear from her first night that something is afoot. The motives are many and the target is clear: Severine herself.

Order your copy here.

You may also be interested in my new historical series, Bright Young Witches. If you are, keep on flipping for a sneak peek.

April 1922

When the Ku Klux Klan appears at the door of the Wode sisters, they decide it's time to visit the ancestral home in England.

With squabbling between the sisters, it takes them too long to realize that their new friend is being haunted. Now they'll have to set aside their fight, discover just why their friend is being haunted, and what they're going to do about it. Will they rid their friend of the ghost and out themselves as witches? Or will they look away?

Join the Wodes as they rise up and embrace just who and what they are in this newest historical mystery adventure.

Order Your Copy Here or keep on scrolling for the first chapter.

SNEAK PEEK OF BRIGHT YOUNG WITCHES & THE RESTLESS DEAD

APRIL 1922. WASHINGTON D.C. USA

ARIADNE EUDORA WISTERIA WODE

"Give me some of the good stuff," the man said, nudging a waiting girl aside. He was wearing a pinstriped evening suit with his hair pomaded back. Given the large ring on his pinky and the gold on his watch chain, Ariadne assumed he was quite wealthy or quite powerful or both. The large cigar hanging from his mouth suggested both.

Ariadne had been just behind him when he went shoving people about and she caught the girl he'd sent stumbling off her bar stool. The height of the girl's heels didn't help, but the man hadn't even noticed he'd knocked the woman down. The girl shot him a nasty, unnoticed look and then turned to Ariadne with a glance that said, *Can you believe this dirty bloke?*

"We're out," the barman said. "Want a Coke?"

The shelves behind him were nearly empty of bottles, unlike the bar itself, which was full. Ariadne sighed. The speakeasy never ordered enough, always ran low, and then the boss took it out on her. He needed either more suppliers, to quit under-ordering, or to open a little less often. Some of the fellows in the bar were reeling drunk and could have been cut off before they'd reached that state. Sloppy drunks put everyone at risk of getting pinched.

"Give me what the management is drinking," the man growled. "I know you got the good stuff, and I don't want any of this second-rate swill that'll leave me blind or dead."

"Our delivery of the good stuff is late," the barman said flatly. Whoever this shove-y man was, the barman was unimpressed. "No one's drinking much until that comes along. Not even the boss man."

Ariadne met the barman's gaze, and he jerked his head to the back. There was a triggerman guarding the door, and the man didn't move when Ariadne approached. His dark eyes fixed on hers, and there was threat in his stony expression.

Here we go again, Ariadne thought, ignoring his look and sliding past him without a flicker of a lash. Posturing was such a gent's move. She had too much to do for this nonsense. When she felt someone watching her, she glanced back and caught the gaze of a bloke with dark, sharp eyes and slicked back hair, with a hefty drink in front of him. He was, she thought, almost certainly a copper. Hopefully he was dirty. Otherwise, they'd all be hauled away with time in the slammer. The goons anyway. The shadows liked Ariadne.

Either way, she wished she was a little less memorable in the drop-waisted, shimmery dress that showed off far more of her chest than she'd prefer. She dressed with the intent to blend in with the other dames. Better to be seen as an easy moll than what she was—a lady-legger. Or, more accurately, a booze-making witch.

"It's about time," Blind Bobby growled as Ariadne appeared. "Do you have it? I don't pay full price for late goods. You're costing me a pile of lettuce, girl."

"They had checkpoints on the way in. I had to think quick and step even more quickly. You're lucky I'm here at all, and you'll be paying me the full amount or I'll take a walk down to the next juice joint. Easy peasy." She snapped her fingers. It was always better not to be too challenging, but sometimes she couldn't help herself.

Blind Bobby put his gun on the table and leaned back. "Maybe I'll just take the booze and pay you nothing, little girl."

"Did you find someone else who makes gin that won't blind you and can age wine and whisky with magic—because I don't think you have found anyone like me."

"I'll pay you eighty percent." He sniffed and growled, "From here on."

His dark, beady eyes fixed on her, and he leaned in, strong jaw gritted. He intended to scare her, but Ariadne was only irritated. She felt as though every time she interacted with this grunting beast, he thought he could just tower over her face and she'd crumple. Ariadne laughed, a trilling thing that didn't sound amused but conveyed her message.

Blind Billy nudged his gun once again, and Ariadne scowled at him, dropping all pretense of amusement. She crossed her arms over her chest and lifted a challenging brow instead. "Do you really want to put a *bean* shooter up against magic?"

"Do you really want to put you and your little sister against my boys? There's even smaller witch brats in that town of yours. What's it called? Nighton? Bring her in." The last was said to one of the apes standing about grasping their guns trying to look intimidating.

There was a sound at the tunnel door and several men poured through with Ariadne's sister, Echo. She struggled in the grasp of...Ariadne's head cocked and gaze narrowed.

Lindsey Noel. She scowled at him. He was the shining son of Nighton and the fellow intent on finding his way into Ariadne's sister Circe's knickers.

"Well, if it isn't Lindsey Noel. Are you joining in on threatening my sisters? *All* of my sisters?"

Lindsey blushed, but his voice was mean. "I know where you live." His fingers dug into Echo's bicep.

"And I know where you live." Ariadne glanced at Echo, who seemed fine despite the white circles under Lindsey's pressing fingers. "Why'd you let them take you?"

"I wanted to see what Lindsey was up to. Sooner or later, Circe will see he's milquetoast playing at being a leading man. She believes that front he puts up, but the mannered handsome puppy will fade into what he really is—another arrogant rube with a rich daddy. It'll go easier if it's me telling her what he did, and after all—he put his hands on me."

Easier, Ariadne translated, than if Ari were the one who told Circe her lover put them all at risk with his playing at being a bad boy.

The idiot Lindsey let go of Echo, but it was too late. The smirk she shot him was enough to have him wondering, would he lose Circe over this? The unfortunate answer was that Ariadne could only wish.

The other men glanced at each other, smirking, when Blind Billy grunted, "No one cares about your hick problems." He gestured and the goons lining the wall leveled their guns at Ariadne.

She sighed. "Until I get paid, you won't be able to open the bottles at the delivery point. Try as you might."

Blind Bobby laughed meanly and Ariadne yawned. He shoved the table back, grabbing his gun as he did, and shoved it into Ariadne's face, pressing it hard against her forehead.

"Careful," she said quietly, "guns do malfunction so easily."

"Open the whiskey, Petey," Blind Billy ordered.

Ariadne rolled her eyes and telepathically told her sister, *Draw your magic.* Ariadne opened her mind and senses to her own magic. She'd originally approached Blind Billy once prohibition went into effect because the church basement where the speakeasy was housed was a place of power. Her magic, always strong, thrummed through her with a vengeance here. Echo's must be a tsunami of power given the dead that even Ariadne could sense.

The ghosts are restless, Echo sent.

Of course they are, it's a desecrated church. How did Noel know about us?

Echo's mental snort seemed to ricochet about Ariadne's head and they both knew the answer: Circe. Soft, trusting, blind-with-love Circe. Lindsey Noel wasn't surprised in the least by their magic. Their sister hated keeping what they were from her 'sweet' Lindsey. She must have talked, and he'd gathered a full confession, given his presence.

Foolish girl.

The grunting of his man trying to open the bottle caught her attention. The goon was yanking at the stopper in the whiskey bottle, desperate to open it. He finally brought out a large knife, but it bounded off of the glass as though it were stone instead of a little bit of cork and glass. Finally he looked up at Blind Billy and shook his head.

Blind Billy pulled the gun back enough just to shove it back against her head again. "That's gonna leave a bruise." His laugh was ugly and he glanced at his men until they were snorting with unbelievable laughter as well.

"Balm of Gilead is an easy enough potion to make for someone like me," Ariadne told him, drawing her magic so deeply that her bobbed hair was slowly starting to rise around her face. "The bruise will be gone in minutes. I carry it in my handbag."

"What about the hole my bullet leaves?" He cocked his gun and then, to her horror, swung his arm wide, aiming at Echo. "Will it cure that?"

"Fool," Ariadne said, finished with this nonsense. She dropped to her knees, covering her head when the gun misfired, and magic rushed into Ariadne as the place of power energized her and she sent the rest of the guns into either misfiring or not firing at all.

With Echo there, ghosts were caught in the energy in the church and within the sisters. The ghosts went mad, merging into a tornado of shadows that sent Blind Billy's goons into shrieking like little girls. Point of fact, Ariadne thought as she started to crawl away from Blind Billy, her little sisters wouldn't have whined like these boys.

A moment later, the copper from earlier rushed the door. Ariadne dropped her magic immediately so it seemed that the screaming goons had gone crazy. On her knees, with forced tears, she looked like a victim as she reached for the copper. She screamed to draw his attention to her from Echo. "Help! Help me, please!"

Police swarmed the room, and Ariadne was yanked to her feet by the first copper to reach her. He glanced her over, muttered, "Fool doll," and shoved her behind him.

She shivered and whimpered and thanked the whole of the group repetitively with big crocodile tears, backing towards the wall. Her dress, her mussed makeup, and her tears were enough for the blokes to not realize she was one of the criminals. Just another doll caught up with the wrong man. She waited until they were all looking the other way, wrestling the goons down, and she slid into the shadows, pulling them around her.

The coppers didn't know about the escape tunnel where Echo had already disappeared, followed by Lindsey Noel. Echo had sealed it against any but Ariadne, so the fuzz were gathering up the men who couldn't use their tunnel while she slipped through, cloaked in darkness and magic.

Using the athamé in her handbag, Ariadne carved a rune of the door to keep it locked. She ignored the skittering of rats and the cool touch of the dead as she hurried down the tunnel.

"Go back to sleep," she murmured to the dead, hoping they'd comply. Otherwise the boys who worked for Blind Billy would find themselves chilled in body and spirit.

The old church had a crypt underneath, so it was better not to look into the dark entrances of side rooms if you wanted to avoid looking at the remnants of the living. The tunnels went from the crypt to beyond the graveyard behind the church, following beneath the road. Blind Billy's men had extended the tunnels even farther. With that kind of work ethic, what might those goons have been capable of if they bothered working for good?

Ariadne mocked herself—knowing she was a criminal too—and moved quickly through the tunnels. There were exits for a good mile down the tunnel road if you knew where to look and what to look for.

The vast majority of Ariadne's booze delivery was still in the auto garage where one of the exits from the tunnels led. The bottles were loaded on the back of her truck. Echo already had their truck running and was just loading the last of the whiskey bottles that had been previously unloaded. Any speakeasy could make gin in their bathtub. Magically aged liqueurs, wines, and whiskey required a witch, a different country, or a very expensive operation that risked prison time. Ariadne sealed the tunnel behind her with the same rune she'd used before. Someone would have to find the runes she'd used and destroy them before the exit would open. Otherwise it would take hours for the spell to fade.

She looked away from her spell and eyed her sister. Echo looked a little mussed but none the worse for wear. "Anyone left here?"

"Just Timmy," Echo grunted as she grabbed the bag of their clothes from behind the truck's seat. "Poor boy. My spell got him hard in the gut when he tried to dodge. He'll have sore ribs if Blind Billy doesn't kill him for losing us and the booze."

"Did Lindsey get out?" Ariadne asked as she shimmied out of her evening gown. Echo tossed Ariadne a wool skirt and blouse, and they stripped down in the auto garage, changing from party clothes to one step away from an initiate for a nunnery.

"He got out when I did, but he was bright enough not to follow me here. We need to consider a change of employment. If things had gone differently, Circe would be raising Medea and Cassiopeia. I love Circe, but…"

Ariadne winced. It was true. If there had been more coppers or if the fellows were a little more trigger happy, they'd have been in trouble. With enough guns blazing, even witches wouldn't have survived.

Ariadne told Echo, "Aunt Beatrix said she was interested in taking over. She has more people. That…that… flimflam that just happened to us wouldn't have happened to her. Not with her sons. Jasper and Gerard with those broad shoulders and thick jaws? Let alone their magic? They won't get the same garbage we're getting."

"We'll still get our cut too," Echo reminded Ariadne with a telling glance. "Beatrix promised it when she wanted to take on the work. You engineered the spells for aging the booze like we do, and Beatrix knows it. We have to be careful, Ariadne—at least until Medea and Cassiopeia are older. They're too little to lose you too."

It wasn't Echo's words that convinced Ariadne. It was the memory of the gun being swung her sister's way. If Echo hadn't been prepared for someone to turn their gun on her, if her magic hadn't been inclined towards the dead, if they'd been firing guns haphazardly, if the sisters had been a little less lucky, Ariadne might have lost her sister. No amount of dough was worth that.

Order Your Copy Here.

* 9 7 9 8 6 6 2 7 6 7 6 7 6 *